TWIN SOULS

Rendi Conn

Patrick,
Thanks for Taking
Care of My Mom

Rendi Conn

11/21/11

Twin Souls by Rendi Conn

ISBN 978-1-4507-0997-2

© Copyright 2010 by Rendi Conn

Cover Design by Mike Castaneda

Published by Bush Publishing P.O. Box 692082

Tulsa, Oklahoma 74169-2082

www.BushPublishing.org

Printed in the USA

DEDICATION

This book is dedicated to my husband and daughters for all the sacrifices they made while I spent time writing. They never complained but encouraged me to continue writing in hopes that one day we would see our dreams fulfilled in print. To my niece for being like my very own.

To my mother. She is my rock, my friend, my confidant, my hero. She is always there for me. Without her strength, I would not be who I am today.

To my sister for her unfailing support and to my brother for his humor that keeps me laughing.

For my friend Roger Ward, without his computer knowledge, I would have been in trouble several times.

To my many other friends and family members who have patiently waited for this book to materialize so they can get their copy.

I say this to you: "Thank you for your love, support and encouragement. I love you all."

-Rendi Conn

In Memoriam of Helen Maxine Ponder, Loving Mother, Mother-in-law, Grandmother.

CHAPTER ONE

The body was lying cold and still at the edge of the ocean while the water lapped around the legs, causing the material of the clothing to move with the current. The full moon cast its luminescent glow across the hair, causing it to look like spun gold.

Walking along the beach, Eric had no idea that the events currently going on in his life were nothing compared to what was about to happen. He was deep in thought, trying to figure out why his fiancée broke off their engagement. As he skirted debris that had come in with the tide, he mused that there had been no warning signs, no fights—nothing that could have accounted for this action. She had simply walked into his apartment, stated that it was not working out for them, apologized, and after taking off her engagement ring, she walked out of his apartment and out of his life.

Stepping over pieces of driftwood, he recounted back over the past eleven months since they had become engaged. It was what she had wanted. They had been dating for the past two years, and she had felt that it was time to make a commitment to each other. He had finally agreed and was anxious to get married, but it seemed like every time he brought up the subject of setting a date, she always had an excuse why she couldn't come up with one.

Replaying the past twenty-four hours in his mind, he couldn't come up with any logical explanations. They had gone to the opening of the opera, *La Boèhm*. Afterward they had gone to Mario's, their favorite restaurant, for a late dinner, then back to her place where they discussed wedding plans. Actually, now that he thought about it, *he* had discussed wedding plans. She had seemed a little withdrawn and unresponsive, especially when he asked her if she had decided on a date for the wedding. She said she hadn't been able to decide on one yet. He left her apartment that night with plans to meet for dinner at his apartment the next evening and a promise from her that she would have a definite date in mind.

She arrived at his place promptly at seven wearing a stunning gown of emerald green that clung seductively to her voluptuous body. Her long copper hair was held in place on one side by a pearl comb and cascaded down her back.

As he replayed the moment in his mind, it now seemed that she had been overdressed for breaking an engagement. He wondered now where had she been going and if she had been planning on meeting someone.

Engrossed in thought, he wasn't aware that he had been walking along the edge of the water, or that he was ruining a two hundred dollar pair of Eddie Bauer's and the very expensive pants he was wearing.

He was startled when he tripped over a very large object lying in the sand. As he regained his senses, he was shocked to discover that the object was the body of a woman. Cautiously, he bent down to turn her over and was relieved when she let out a low moan.

Opening her eyes slowly, she stared up at the sky, and turning her head, she looked at him. Finding his voice, he asked her, "Are you okay?" She didn't respond to him and he asked again, "Miss, are you all right?"

As she struggled to sit up she, answered him, "Yes, yes, I think so."

He placed his hands behind her and helped her into a sitting position. Thanking him, she asked, "Where am I?"

"You're at Candlestick Beach. Don't you remember how you got here?" She was certain how she had arrived there, but she couldn't tell this man. He would think she was crazy. Or worse, think she was insane and had escaped from La Grier, the state mental facility that was just twenty-five miles away.

He offered his hand when she attempted to stand.

Accepting it, she stood facing him and, weighing her answer, finally said, "I really don't remember. What time is it?"

A check of his watch surprised him; it was three o'clock in the morning. Still holding onto her arm for fear that she wouldn't be able to stand on her own, he asked, "Were you left here by someone? Do you have a car nearby?"

What could she answer him that he would believe? "No, I don't have a car. I was with some friends earlier."

He studied her for a few seconds wondering if he should offer her a ride, wondering if she would accept one. "Look, my car is parked just up the hill; I could give you a lift."

She normally wasn't in the habit of accepting rides from strangers, but considering her circumstances and her alternatives, she didn't have much of a choice. It was, after all, three in the morning and she was stranded on this beach in the middle of nowhere. Besides, nothing he could possibly do to her would make a difference after what she had already been through tonight. Graciously she accepted his offer. "Please, if it wouldn't be too much of an inconvenience, I really would appreciate one."

As they started to walk up the hill, she stopped. Looking down at her feet, she began to laugh. She had only one shoe on, and the heel was broken off. After a short, futile search for the other shoe, they proceeded up the hill to his car.

When they reached the road, he told her to stand still and that he would run up and get the car from the lot. She watched as he jogged away, admiring the strong, steady gait of his well-muscled legs. She wondered if he jogged regularly, because he had the look of someone who ran.

Waiting for him gave her an opportunity to appraise her situation. Her hair was squalid from the ocean water, and her clothes were caked with drying sand and mud. Her stockings, or what was left of them, had runs, and her toes were sticking out of one foot. She knew without a doubt that she was an unsightly mess.

She was contemplating on what to tell him when he pulled up in front of her. The door opened as she reached for it, and she was embraced with a rush of warm air. Sensing her hesitation, he said, "Come on, I promise it's safe."

She said, "It's not that: I don't want to ruin your car seats."

Shaking his head, he said, "Don't worry about it; the seats will clean. Get in before you catch a cold."

Sliding into the seat, she immediately began to relax and relish the heat. Blushing as she looked over at him, she told him, "I want to thank you for all the help you're giving me.

I really don't know what I would have done if you hadn't been here."

"No problem. I'm just glad I was there to help. I am always willing to help a damsel in distress. Look, I know it isn't my business, but if you want to talk about it, I'm a great listener."

"Actually, there really isn't much to tell. I was with some friends earlier this evening, and obviously, the night ended up badly because I ended up out here. I don't want to sound unappreciative or rude, especially since you are being so kind to help me, but that really is about all I can tell you."

"Hey, that's quite all right. You only tell me what you want me to know. You don't owe me any explanations. This is a free ride, no hidden costs. Fair enough?"

Smiling shyly at him, she answered, "Fair enough. By the way, my name is Jerica Zimmerman."

Returning her smile with one of his own, he said, "Nice to meet you, Jerica. My name is Eric Hansen. Now, where's home?"

After Jerica gave Eric her address, she sat back and took in her surroundings. The car was a silver Lexus with burgundy and gray velour interior. The computerized voice on the control panel talked when it needed to advise the driver of any problems such as an open door, or to remind passengers to buckle their seatbelts. It even told the driver when to refuel.

She must have dozed off because the sound of his voice startled her.

Apologizing and embarrassed, she told him, "I'm sorry. I guess the heat and all relaxed me so much I dozed off." She looked up and realized they were in her driveway. She became more embarrassed because it dawned on her that she had been asleep for most of the ride. Smiling sheepishly at him, she said, "Well, I want to thank you for the ride home. I hope this hasn't been too much of an inconvenience for you. Could I pay you for your time and gas?"

"It will be a sad day when a man can't come to the aid of a beautiful damsel in distress out of the goodness of his heart. No money is necessary, but I would like to call you later just to see how you are, if that is all right with you."

Surprised and quite pleased, she agreed. "Sure, that would be fine." Eric pulled a pen and paper from the glove compartment and handed it to her. Smiling at him, she jotted down her telephone number and gave it to him. Stepping out of the car, she thanked him again for all his help. Waving, she ran up the steps of the porch.

Eric watched her go safely inside before he pulled out of the driveway. He decided he would definitely call her later. There was a mystery about Jerica Zimmerman, and he wanted to know what it was. His curiosity was piqued; her beauty and mystery had captured his interest.

On the drive to his apartment, he wondered about her. What had she been doing on the beach at this hour? Had she been on a date, gotten into an argument, and then left there? Had she been drinking? Drugs? No, she didn't look the type. Even wet and disheveled as she had been, he could tell that her clothing had been of fine quality and probably expensive.

He was sure that whatever the reason, it couldn't have been of her own accord. Considering the situation, she had handled herself very well. Most people in that position would have been hysterical. From the first moment he had stumbled onto her, she was calm and in complete control of her emotions.

CHAPTER TWO

Jerica stepped into the house and leaned against the front door. Looking up, she saw her brother sitting in his favorite recliner. He wasn't at all surprised to see his sister in the state she was in. He simply looked at his watch, made a few notes in his notebook, and smiled at her.

Jerica sat down in the chair nearest her brother. "Justin, you have got to stop doing this to me!"

Giving his sister a big grin he said, "I knew you could do it. You always do."

Shaking her head at her brother, "True, I always have before, but what if I hadn't this time? How would you have felt? What then, Justin?" Getting up from his chair, he knelt beside his sister.

Taking her hands in his, he told her, "It won't happen again. It is just that you have always made it before, and I knew you would this time. However, you are right. I couldn't handle it if anything happened to you. I'll quit. This was the last time."

Jerica looked at her brother's face, which was like looking at her own. "Justin, I know that the last few times were successful. I can't deny that, but somehow this time was different. I really can't explain why, except that usually when I come around, I know where I am and what happened. Tonight I was really disoriented. I didn't know where I was or what had happened.

"Then it finally came to me that you were up to your old tricks again. I also felt cold. It wasn't just because I was wet either. This was a funny cold. Like I was not real anymore. It was almost like emptiness. It was almost as if...I was dead.

"Please Justin, no more."

Rising from her chair, she rumpled her brother's hair. "I'm going to take a long hot shower, and then I'm going to bed."

She was halfway down the hall when her brother called to her. Coming up to his sister, he gave her a big hug. "I love you, sis. I won't ever let anything happen to you. Go take your shower, then get some rest. I'll have a pot of strong, hot coffee waiting for you when you get up."

He watched as his sister closed the bathroom door. He stood deep in thought like that until he heard the water begin to run. Then he returned to the living room and to his notes.

It was sometime later when he heard the water shut off and Jerica's bedroom door open, then close. Taking up his pen again, he continued with his notes. He worked for a long time when he suddenly jumped from his chair. "Jerica was right! This wasn't like all the other times." By his calculations, it had taken Jerica approximately five hours and seventeen minutes to return. He was not sure, of course, because he was going by the time she arrived at home versus the time he began.

After doing some more calculations, he guessed that it had taken approximately three hours longer than before. *Maybe Jerica is right, maybe it is time to quit*, he thought. There was no mistaking the evidence. This time had been different than the others. Stretching and yawning, he rose from the chair and decided to call it a night. Turning off the kitchen light, he went down the hall. Stopping outside of Jerica's room, he eased open the door just enough to peek inside and make sure that she was all right. She seemed to be resting comfortably. Quietly closing the door, he went to his own room.

Tired as he was, sleep was elusive. He was concerned that it had taken longer for her to return. At first, it had been almost instantaneous, and then it had become a little longer each time. The longest time to this point was about an hour to two hours, but it had never taken five hours.

After about an hour of restlessness, he fell into an exhausted slumber only to awaken from a terrible nightmare. He was covered in perspiration, and his bedclothes were soaked. He dreamed that Jerica had actually failed to make it back, and it frightened him. Deciding that sleep had escaped him for the rest of the night, he sat on the edge of the bed, rubbing his head. He stepped into his slippers, pulled on his robe, and went to the kitchen to make a pot of coffee.

Filling his cup, he sat down at the kitchen table. He watched out the bay window as the sun was just beginning to come up over the treetops. It was a magnificent sunrise, tinged with pink and the slightest hint of blue. It looked like it was going to be a beautiful day.

Picking up his notebook and reading the night's events, he set about refilling his coffee cup. He was so engrossed in his reading he forgot that he was pouring coffee until it splattered on the floor. Jumping up, he grabbed a dishtowel to clean up his mess. As he was bending over, a sharp flash of pain seared through his head, blurring his vision.

Slumping to the floor, Justin grabbed his head with both hands. When his vision cleared and he was able to stand up, he finished cleaning up the floor. Going down the hall to the bathroom, he searched in the medicine cabinet for something to ease his headache.

Taking two long capsules from a bottle, he filled a glass with water. Looking at himself in the mirror, he saw he was pale and there were dark circles under his eyes.

He hoped this wasn't the beginning of those awful headaches again. It seemed like they were getting worse instead of better.

By the time he finished dressing for work, his headache had begun to subside. He was hoping that he would have the lab all to himself today, especially since he really didn't feel like going in.

As he was heading to the kitchen to get his notes, the telephone rang. He was surprised to hear a male voice ask for his sister. Gently putting the receiver down, he went to awaken her.

"Jerica, wake up. You have a phone call. It's a man." Making sure that she was fully awake, he went to hang up the other telephone. As he pulled her door shut, he heard her answer the call, "Hello?"

"Jerica, hi. This is Eric. Did I wake you?"

"Yes, but that's okay. I probably should have been up long ago. What time is it?"

"It's about 12:15 PM. Have you recovered from last night?"

"Well, yes, actually, I think I have, or at least will have by the time I get my coffee. Did you manage to get any rest?"

"Yes, a little. I even got up at eight-thirty this morning and went jogging. Listen, I know we just met and all, but I was wondering if you would have dinner with me tonight? I know this is short notice, so I'll understand if you say no."

Surprised, Jerica eagerly accepted. "Yes, I would love to have dinner with you tonight, but on one condition…that we have seafood." Laughing, she continued, "For some reason, I have this enormous craving for seafood."

Sharing her humor, he replied, "Seafood it is. You've got yourself a date. I'll pick you up at seven if that is okay with you."

"Seven it is then. I'm looking forward to it. And Eric, thanks again for the help last night. See you then." Hanging up, she donned her robe and slippers, and humming a tune to herself, she went to the kitchen in search of the hot coffee her brother had promised her.

Entering the kitchen, she not only found the coffee as promised but also a delicious breakfast of bacon, eggs, biscuits, and gravy awaiting her. "Hey, big brother, what is all this? This looks great!"

Taking her place at the table, her brother came over and kissed her on the cheek. "Well, since you don't recognize it, it is called breakfast. Besides, I don't recall it being a crime to cook one's own sister breakfast. I'm not afraid of being arrested or anything like that, so why don't you just shut up and eat."

Playfully punching at him, she scooped up a spoonful of eggs and plopped them onto her plate. "Well, crime or no crime, I wouldn't mind this becoming a habit."

Jerica was the one who usually prepared their breakfast. She enjoyed getting up early and watching the sunrise while bacon sizzled in the pan. When she was a little girl, she had shared many a morning like that with her mother. It was a special time for them to talk just between mother and daughter.

"This really is good, Justin. Thanks for making this for us." "No problem. I figure I needed to eat something since I am getting one of my infamous migraines again. It woke me, and since I couldn't go back to sleep, I decided to stay up and do some work."

Looking at her brother, she realized that he did look ill. Leaning over, she felt his forehead. He seemed a little feverish. "Have you taken your temperature this morning or any medication?"

"I took two aspirin this morning but not my temperature. I was planning on going to the lab today, but I think I'll just stay home."

"I think you should, too. Besides, it's Saturday. It's not as if you have to go in."

"I know, but I started some new work yesterday, and I need to talk to Jim about it. I need to check on its growth today."

"Well, then call Jim and let him take care of it. I'm sure he is perfectly capable of watching fungus grow." Rinsing her plate off, she said, "I think you should get some rest instead of burning up the notebooks today. You know how you get when those headaches hit. I'm going to the mall to buy myself a new dress. I have a date with Eric tonight."

"Eric? Could that be our mystery gentleman caller this morning?"

Jerica grinned, "It could be. I met him last night. Actually, he is the one who found me lying on the beach where you left me. He wanted to call this morning to see if I was all right. He asked me to dinner tonight, and since he was so kind to help me last night, I accepted. Of course, the fact that he is absolutely gorgeous has nothing to do with it."

Returning her grin, Justin said, "Oh, of course not. Why would good looks be a factor in accepting a dinner invitation? Anyway, why didn't you tell me that someone else found you? What did you tell him? What reason did you give him for being out there at that hour of the night?"

Jerica could tell that this had upset her brother. "Calm down. I didn't tell him anything. I mean, what could I tell him? Oh, I guess I could have said, 'Oh, this is no big deal. My brother just tries to kill me on a regular basis!' Be realistic, Justin. I just told him that I had been out with some friends and the night had ended badly. I am sure he didn't believe it, but he was too much of a gentleman to press the issue. Now I need to get dressed. I have to run a ton of errands today."

"Wait, sis. I'm sorry. I shouldn't have been so rough on you. It's just that this thing with you is so unique, and I'm afraid for you. I would like to ask you a few more questions if you're not too angry to answer them."

Sitting back down at the table, she told him to go ahead. He wanted to know everything she could remember. What time it was when she finally came around, how she felt, and what was the first thing she thought about.

"Well, let's see, I remember coming into my bedroom to get my purse before I left, and someone grabbed me from behind. I guess that was you. What in the world did you put over my face anyway? It smelled like an old pair of gym socks! Then I don't remember anything else until Eric found me on the beach and I asked him what time it was, and he said it was three in the morning.

Then he helped me to his car and brought me home. I was afraid to take the ride because I didn't want to ruin his upholstery, since I was a wet and muddy mess. Did you have to use the ocean, Justin? You ruined a very expensive dress, not to mention my new shoes! If the dry cleaners can't clean it, my love, you are going to owe me a new dress."

"It will be worth a new dress if I can come up wth the answers we need. Shoot! I'll buy you a whole new wardrobe! Now I think I'll go lie down. My headache doesn't seem to be letting up. In fact, it seems to be a little worse. While you're in town today, would you please stop by the drug store and get me a bottle of aspirin? I took the last two this morning." Picking up his notebook, he headed toward his room.

In his room, he sat down at his desk. Although this test had been different, his sister didn't seem any worse the wear for it. Still, he had a strange feeling this test had been a turning point in his research, and in their lives as well. He made a mental note to look into the fact that it had taken longer for her to recover. He felt that somehow that was the key to all of this. His headache had come to a full migraine again and was dulling his concentration. He put the book down and crawled into his bed.

CHAPTER THREE

Promptly at seven, the doorbell rang. In a flurry of excitement, Jerica hurried to open the door. Eric was hiding behind a large bouquet of flowers. As he handed her the flowers, their eyes met and the intensity of the gleam in his eyes caused her heart to flutter. Breaking the spell she said, "Wow, it's a good thing I answered the door instead of Justin. I would hate to have to fight him over these flowers. They are beautiful."

Eric's eyes gleamed with appreciation as he took in her appearance. She wore a low cut dress of blue velvet that was split up the right side and clung seductively to her figure.

Her honey-golden hair was piled high on her head with a few strands hanging down for effect. She wore her most precious jewelry, a diamond necklace in the shape of a heart, with matching earrings. They had belonged to her mother, and she only wore them on very special occasions.

"You look wonderful!"

"Thank you, Eric. Won't you please come in. I would like you to meet my brother Justin. Justin, this is Eric Hansen, the gentleman who gave me the ride home last night."

Accepting the hand that Eric proffered, he said, "Nice to meet you. I also want to thank you for helping my sister out last night. She told me how kind you were to her."

"No thanks needed. It was my pleasure." Looking at Jerica, he noticed a slight color had heightened her cheeks. He found her modesty a refreshing change from Donna, who had always thrived on having compliments given to her.

Excusing herself, she went to the kitchen to find a vase for the flowers. From the sound of the conversation coming from the living room, she could tell that Justin and Eric were quickly becoming friends. They had already managed to change the conversation from her to football.

Coming back into the room, she heard her brother ask, "Where are you two going for dinner? That is, if you don't mind my asking."

"No, not at all. I made reservations for us at Pelican's Wharf."

Interrupting, Jerica said, "Eric is being kind to me. I was craving seafood for some strange reason, and he decided to indulge me." Winking at her brother, she knew he would catch the underlying joke, but for different reasons.

Standing, Eric said that they had better be going because their reservations were for eight.

A little past eight they were being led to their table. The maître d' admired Jerica's beauty and winked approvingly to Eric. Nodding an agreement, he seated Jerica. After taking their drink orders, he winked once more, then hurried away.

The restaurant was a picture book setting. Their table was in the balcony overlooking the bay. A liquid moon melted gold across the water, illuminating everything in its path. A ship could be seen in the distance. Its lights mirrored on the darkened waters, displaying a lovely array of colors.

"Oh look! Isn't it lovely? It has always been one of my dreams to take a cruise, and one of these days I intend to fulfill it. What about you? Have you ever taken a cruise?" she asked.

Laughing he answered, "No, I've never been on a ship before. I can just imagine all the dining, dancing, drinks, late night parties, with splitting hangovers the next morning. Now that would be great!"

Imagining Eric with an ice pack on his head, she laughed. "Yeah, that does sounds great."

Just then, the maître d' arrived with their drinks. Jerica allowed Eric to order for them, and his choices were excellent.

Lobster bisque was served steaming hot, followed by shrimp scampi and cracked crab. Jerica ate heartily until the smoked squid arrived. Wrinkling her nose, she politely declined, although Eric tried to persuade her into it.

Dessert was cherries jubilee, and they both indulged in a healthy portion. Having finished their meal, their hunger sated, Eric escorted her to the lounge where a small, intimate band was playing.

Pulling her into his arms, he asked her if she would like to dance.

"After what I just ate, it would be a good way to exercise it off."

They made an attractive couple. They drew admiring glances from many of the other guests. His dark, good looks complimented her fair, blonde beauty.

Upon leaving the restaurant, he suggested a drive. He was reluctant to let the night end because he was enjoying her company.

They drove out to Myers Lake. Leaving the car, they walked the path that surrounded the lake. The moon cast its light upon the rippling water as a gentle breeze blew across the waves. The beauty of the night made a perfect ending to a wonderful date. Never before had Jerica enjoyed a man's company as much as she was enjoying Eric's. He was a most witty and charming escort. She didn't want the night to end.

Wanting to know more about him, she asked, "What line of work do you do Eric?"

"I'm in the legal profession. Actually, I'm an attorney."

"That's wonderful. What firm are you with?"

Grinning sheepishly, Eric admitted that he was in a partnership with his father. "Hansen and Hansen. Our offices are downtown in the Commercial Towers Building."

Jerica was impressed. When she had been introduced to him, she hadn't made the connection. Hansen and Hansen was one of the most affluent law firms in the city, and Eric's reputation preceded him. She smiled to herself. His modesty was refreshing. Most men in his position would have been more than a little taken with themselves. She definitely knew her share of attorneys, and that had been her impression of most of them. Especially the young ones just out of school, who carried an air of arrogance about them.

"Now, enough about me. What about you? Where does Jerica earn her bread and butter?"

"Well, my life isn't as exciting as yours. I am a CPA with a downtown firm. I have been with them for nine years. I live with my brother Justin, whom you have met, and our cat Charlie, whom, if you have the privilege to meet, you will never forget.

"He is one of those cats that leave you with a lasting impression. He is a big, ugly tomcat. He has half of his right ear missing. He got into a fight with the Jacobs' pit bull next door. Charlie lost. It took Justin and me two months to get him healed. Every time we got his ear wrapped, Charlie would go out and get into another scrape and we would have to start all over again. We decided to just lock him up, and after five days, we finally had to let him out in self-defense. He pretty much drove us crazy between his whining to be let outside and his clawing everything up he could get near. See, like I said, I don't live a very exciting life. I imagine you could tell me a story more interesting than one about an ugly tomcat."

Laughing, Eric assured her that none could compare to hers. "You never said what firm you were with?"

"Oh, Danforth and Jones. Ever heard of them?"

Now it was Eric's turn to be impressed. "You're kidding! I know that firm very well. They are one of our best clients. We do work for them regularly. As for you not living a very exciting life, I wouldn't agree on that one entirely. I would say last night bordered on exciting. It isn't every night that I get to stumble over a beautiful woman lying on the beach at three in the morning. I hope you don't think I'm prying, but my curiosity has gotten the better of me. I really want to know how you ended up at the beach last night."

How could she tell him that her brother had tried to kill her? He wouldn't understand. She didn't even think that he would believe her. Biting her lip she told him, "I know that last night was strange.

"There really isn't anyway I can explain to you what happened without sounding insane. The best explanation I can give you is the same as last night. It was a night that ended badly. I hope you understand."

He didn't understand, but he assured her that he did. Something was very wrong here, and he wanted to know what it was. He had the strangest feeling that Jerica was in some sort of danger, and he didn't like that feeling. "Okay, no more questions about last night."

It was getting late, and he knew he should be getting her home. It was with some reluctance that he said they should be going.

Pulling into her driveway, he turned to her, "I had a great time. I would like to see you again."

Smiling, she agreed that she also had a great time. "I would like to see you again, too. I haven't had this much fun in a long time."

Running around to help her out of the car, he pulled her into his arms. Unable to resist the urge to kiss her, his mouth covered hers. As their tongues met, the intensity of the kiss surprised them both. Embarrassed and a little ashamed of herself, she pulled away. She was shivering, but it wasn't from being cold. Thanking him again, she went into the house.

Eric watched until she was safely inside, then pulled away and headed for home.

Stepping inside, Jerica leaned weakly against the door. Eric's kiss had left her shaky.

Looking up from his book, her brother asked, "How was your date?"

Smiling, she sat down on the couch next to him. "You know, I don't believe in love at first sight, but after tonight I do believe there is such a thing as 'intense like' at first sight."

Grinning at his sister he said, "I take it that all went well."

She kissed her brother's cheek. Looking back over her shoulder as she headed down the hallway, she called to him. "That is an understatement, big brother! I had a marvelous time!"

Justin could hear her singing as she readied herself for bed. He hadn't seen her this happy since they were fifteen and their parents had gotten her the horse that she had been wanting ever since she had seen the movie *Black Beauty*. Putting away his book, he made sure the front door was locked, turned off the lights, and decided to call it a night.

CHAPTER FOUR

Monday morning found Jerica out of bed and dressed in a hurry. She had a big day ahead of her. The new client that was coming in today was a multi-million dollar corporation. If she impressed the president of the company, then she could secure the contract for all their accounting.

Dressed in a navy blue suit, she knew she looked good. The image looking back at her from the mirror was one of a confident, professional woman. She felt as if she could tackle the world and win. Her walk was sure and light as she went down the hall to the kitchen.

She was surprised to see the kitchen empty. Normally, Justin would be up working on his second pot of coffee. He liked to get up early and do some work before heading to the lab.

Jerica prepared the coffeepot, then deciding on muffins and fresh fruit for breakfast, she went outside to get the morning newspaper.

Stepping out on the porch, she was not surprised to see Charlie run past her. He would stay out all night, but come morning he was ready for his breakfast, then a long, restful nap, only to be ready to leave again at dark to roam the neighborhood.

Opening a can of cat food, she asked him, "What kind of mischief did you get into last night?" Emptying the can into his bowl, she scratched him behind his ear.

Breakfast was almost ready when she realized that Justin had not gotten up yet. Going to his bedroom, she knocked on his door. "Hey sleepy head, you going to get up today or do you plan on making this a new career move? Breakfast is ready."

Hearing him mumble, she opened the door and went inside. Her brother was lying on his bed, and it was apparent that he was ill. Placing her hand on his forehead, she was startled to find him burning up. "Justin, you have a very high fever. What's wrong? Do you hurt anywhere?"

Sitting up and holding his head with both hands, he told her that he had one of his migraines again. "Sis, would you please get me some aspirin? They are in the medicine cabinet. My head feels like it is about to explode."

Hurrying to the bathroom, she rummaged through the cabinet until she found what she was looking for. Shaking two into the palm of her hand, she filled a glass with water and hurried to Justin's room.

Swallowing the tablets, he laid back down. Jerica advised him to stay in bed and she would call him later to see how he was doing.

"I'll be fine. Go eat your breakfast, then get out of here before you're late. You mother hen! I promise to be a good little boy today."

Smiling to let his sister know that he would be fine, he assured her that he would take it easy. "Now get going. You have that big meeting today, and you don't need to be worrying about me. Go. Knock 'em dead!"

Kissing her brother's cheek, she admonished him to stay in bed. Leaving his room, she went to the kitchen.

She was worried about her brother. She didn't like it when he got these headaches. He used to be the stronger of the two. When they were children, she had always been the sickly one. Their mother used to put them in the same room in hopes that they would both get the illness at the same time and get it over with. Usually Justin managed to evade whatever it was that she was afflicted with. He would be up playing while she was lying in bed miserable.

Justin had been relatively healthy up until he was sixteen. Then he started getting headaches. His sister was worried about him because it had been awhile since he had one of these headaches. Now it seemed as if they were back in full force.

She decided that if he was not better by the time she arrived home from work, he was going to go see Doc Fletcher. He had been their family doctor since they had moved to the city, about ten years ago. He usually gave Justin a prescription for pain medicine to help ease his headaches. The doctor had run every test imaginable but couldn't come up with a logical, medical reason for the headaches. His best diagnosis was stress, related to Justin's work.

Arriving at work, Jerica was surprised to find a stack of messages already waiting on her desk. At the bottom of the stack was a message from Eric. She smiled to think he had called her so early. Unfortunately, she did not have the time to return the call. She had to hurry if she was going to make her meeting. It would not do to keep the president of a multi-million-dollar company waiting.

Gathering her files together for her presentations, she was just about to leave her office when the telephone rang. Thinking that it might be her boss with some last minute instructions, she grabbed the telephone.

"Jerica. Hi, it's Eric."

Looking at the clock, she said, "Good morning."

"Look, I know it's early and you probably have some important client waiting, so I'll make this brief. I just wanted to know if you would go out with me this Friday. I really had a great time and would like to repeat it."

"I would love to. Oh no, wait, I can't. I have a dinner to attend, unless you would like to accompany me to that? It probably won't be very much fun. The company is hosting this dinner to honor all the prominent clients that we currently service. I'm sure the food will be a treat, though. The president of this company always hires the best caterers.

"It is a black tie affair, which means getting all dressed up. I don't usually mind these parties. It is only once a year, and besides, it is the only time I get a chance to spend an evening with a bunch of overrated, over dressed, rich, plastic people."

Laughing at her description of this dinner party, he said he couldn't help but accept the invitation. "I'll go, but on one condition. You make it up to me on Saturday. I'll make it a treat. We can go to McDonald's or Burger King. I'll let you choose."

Jerica's bright and melodious laugh sent shivers all over him. He loved the sound of it. She said, "It's a date. Sorry to cut this short, but I have to be in a meeting in about zero seconds. Call me tonight and we can discuss definite plans." After saying their good byes, she cradled the phone, grabbed her presentation, and quickly ran down the hall to the elevator with a prayer that it wouldn't be stopping on every floor.

Taking a deep breath and saying a quick prayer, she entered the conference room, greeted her client, Mr. Hoffmier, and the meeting began.

CHAPTER FIVE

Jerica arrived home feeling elated. Her meeting with Mr. Hoffmier went fantasticly. He had been so impressed by her that he immediately accepted her proposal. He gave her the account right on the spot, agreeing to meet every one of her demands regarding salary and control of the company's accounts. Her reputation had preceded her, and Hoffmier knew after one look at her that his accounts were safe and she could be trusted.

Jerica was a professional who was in complete control of her life. She knew what she had to offer and didn't back down. Hoffmier admired those qualities in a person. In today's society, so few people portrayed the confidence that she did. He liked her youth and ambition. He left the meeting fully satisfied that his company would be taken good care of.

As Jerica walked through the front door of the house, her excitement died. Justin was lying on the floor unconscious. Terrified, she screamed, "Justin! Justin, wake up!" After several frightful moments, he finally came to.

Helping him sit up she asked, "What happened?"

Holding his head in his hands, he told his sister what he could remember. "I was sitting in my chair doing some reading and had the TV on. Someone came to the door. I got up to answer it, and I remember feeling dizzy... and that's it. Until now."

"Do you have any idea how long you were lying there?"

"No, none. I was reading and watching some movie on television. I had no idea what time it was."

Jerica was afraid her brother could have injured himself when he fell. She was also upset that he had been lying there unconscious by himself. As she walked to the telephone and began dialing, she said, "I'm calling Doc Fletcher."

Justin immediately followed her and took the telephone out of her hand. "No, you're not. I'm fine now. It was just one of my headaches. I probably should have taken some more aspirin."

Looking at him incredulously, she asked, "You really don't believe that, do you, Justin?"

Hanging up the telephone, he said, "Yes, I do. Quit making a big deal of this. Look, if this happens again, I'll call old Doc Fletcher myself. Now, can't we drop this? Really, I am all right."

"No, I don't want to drop this, but I can see that I'm getting nowhere with you, so I'll let it go. But rest assured I will bring up the subject again."

Shaking his head at his sister, he said, "Fine. Subject change—what's for dinner? I'm starving."

After a hug, they went to the kitchen to see what Jerica could prepare for dinner. She made him some chicken soup, hot rolls, and cheese wedges. For dessert, they had a delicious, homemade apple pie that one of the ladies at Jerica's office had made for her and brought her just this morning. She sliced off two good-sized pieces, and placing one in front of her brother, she was pleased to see him indulge himself.

She felt a little bit better about her brother after seeing that his appetite had not suffered. In fact, he ate as if he had not eaten in a couple of days. Hopefully that was a good sign.

Justin felt decidedly better after he had eaten. He wanted his sister to tell him how her meeting had gone that morning with Hoffmier. After telling her brother about the meeting, she could see the look of pride and admiration come to his eyes. She knew he was proud of her. Even as children, when she had accomplished something, Justin was the first to congratulate her.

"Way to go, sis! I knew you would have them eating out of the palm of your hand."

Giving her brother a playful kick under the table, she teased him that she was definitely getting a prejudiced opinion.

The next morning Justin was up early. He was preparing breakfast when Jerica came in. Setting a cup of coffee in front of his sister, he noticed her look of surprise.

"Good morning, sister dear. Sleep well?"

"Yeah, I did. And from the looks of it, so did you. I take it that you are feeling much better today?"

"Yeah, I am. In fact, my headache is now only a dull throb. It is so slight, it's almost non-existent. So quit worrying about me and pass the sugar."

Passing him the antique sugar bowl, she told him of her plans. "I'll be a little late tonight. I have to stop by the cleaners and pick up our clothes. I have to go to the store for a few things. Can you think of anything we need?"

While spreading jam on his toast, he asked her what was she getting from the store.

"Let me see... butter, eggs, milk, bread, some fresh fruits, and some laundry detergent. Can you think of anything I forgot?"

"You better get some more bacon. I just cooked the last of it. Also, pick me up another notebook—you know the kind I use."

Jotting bacon down on her list, she said, "Justin, you must literally sit around and do nothing but scribble on all those pages with as many notebooks as you go through. I'll pick up a few of them for you. Maybe that will hold you for awhile, you think?"

Getting up from the table, she scraped her plate into the trash. Washing her dishes and leaving them in the drain, she told him that she would see him later.

After she left, Justin got up and washed his dishes as well. He was still feeling a little weak. Grabbing his notebook, he made a few notations in it, then he retrieved his briefcase and left for work.

CHAPTER SIX

Justin worked for Howard Pharmaceuticals. He was chief scientist over the experimental laboratory. He spent most of his days working on experiments, trying to cure one disease after another. The project they had him working on at the present was classified as "Top Secret." Justin loved his work, and he was good at it. He had been trying one experiment after another ever since he was a child. He had won two Nobel Prizes for the discovery of two vaccines.

He found that today, however, his concentration level was surprisingly low. He attributed it to being sick the past few days. He barely managed to make it through the day. When he was finally able to break free, he found that he was more than ready to go home. It had been a long day.

Both Justin and Jerica arrived home at the same time. Getting out of the car, Jerica went to retrieve the mail. Walking back up the driveway, she yelled at her brother to give her a hand with the groceries.

Opening the front door, Justin pushed his briefcase inside and turned to help his sister. Grabbing a couple of sacks of groceries, he went inside. After carrying in the six bags of stuff she had purchased, he flopped down in his favorite chair and asked, "I thought you only had a few items to buy. What did you do? Buy the store out?"

Laughing, she admitted that once she got started she could not seem to stop. "For every one item I bought, I found two items to go with it.

Before I knew it, I had spent $198. We won't have to go shopping again for another month."

Getting up to see what his sister had purchased, he told her he would help her put the groceries away. He noticed that she had bought most of his favorite foods. He knew she was spoiling him because he had been sick. That was something they had done for each other ever since they were small.

Once, Jerica had fallen from their tree house and had broken her leg. Justin had taken some of his money from his savings account and bought her a new dress that she had been wanting.

He remembered the look on her face when he handed her the exquisitely wrapped package. She had been so pleased that she almost ripped his head off hugging him so hard.

After the cast had been removed from her leg, he had taken her to one of the school dances so she could show off her new dress. Since she had been out of classes because of her leg, she didn't have a date for the dance, and all the boys already had dates. All her friends had been envious of her. She had looked so beautiful, and most of the boys had spent the evening talking to her.

Shaking himself out of his reverie, he asked, "Well, since we have such an array of food to choose from, what are we going to have for dinner?"

"Believe it or not, I'm not real hungry after doing all that shopping. I am more tired than anything else. How does something light sound to you?"

He agreed with his sister. While she went to change her clothes, he started pulling dishes from the cabinet.

She came back wearing a pair of faded, old jeans and one of her brother's sweatshirts. She prepared them a small chef salad, fresh melon, and bran muffins with honey butter.

They ate their meal in companionable silence. Each of them was unaware that their thoughts were traveling on the same plane; they were thinking about Friday night. She, of course, was thinking about Eric, and he was thinking about the test. They both began to speak at the exact same moment.

"Justin."

"Jerica."

They both laughed and she motioned him to go ahead.

"Well, I was just thinking of the test. I was trying to figure out why it took you so long to return this time. I want to know why this test was so different from the last one. I was wondering if maybe it was the nature of the test. Or maybe it was the elements involved."

"Look, Justin, I don't have any more answers than you do. I can't even begin to understand any of this myself. If I were to stop long enough to understand it, I would probably end up in a rubber room bouncing off the walls. The only thing I can figure is that somehow, during the car accident, something was triggered to set this off. There can't be any other explanation as far as I can see, since that was the first time we realized there was something going on. All I know is that this test was different, and it scared me. If it hadn't been for Eric and all the help he gave me that night, I don't know where I would have ended up."

Smiling at her, he said, "Eric, oh yeah, I almost forgot about him. So tell me, little sister, what is the story on him, and when do you plan to see him again?"

Jerica told him about the telephone call that morning and that he was going to escort her to her company dinner.

"Well, I can tell by the look on your face and the tone of your voice that this guy has definitely gotten your attention. Why else would you give him my job of escorting you to that dinner?"

Mortified, she looked at her brother, "Oh Justin, I'm so sorry. I completely forgot that you were taking me. I'll call him right now and explain it to him."

"Whoa, hold the phone little sister. No way am I going to let you do that. Are you kidding? He is saving me from a fate worse than death. You know how I hate dressing up in that monkey suit and socializing with all those rich, eccentric snobs. This is my chance to run. In fact, give me the phone so I can call and thank him."

Playfully punching her brother, she said, "I'm sorry I forgot. I know you never did like going to these affairs, and I do appreciate all the times you did take me. If you're sure that you are not mad, then I'll wash and you dry. Come on, clown. Let's clean up our dinner mess."

Grabbing the towel, she snapped it at her brother and then squealed when he took it from her and chased her into the living room trying to pop her with it.

CHAPTER SEVEN

Eric was sitting in his dining room looking out over the ocean. It was late, and sleep had been elusive. It had only been five days since he first stumbled onto Jerica, but she had managed to occupy almost every minute of his thoughts. He sure wasn't acting like a man whose fiancée had just dumped him. In fact, he had not given Donna more than an occasional thought this past week. Maybe now was the time to try to sort out what had happened between them.

He picked up the telephone, and after dialing the first three digits of her number, he hung up. No, he wasn't going to call her. She was the one who walked out, and it was up to her to make the first move.

Besides, Eric needed more time to sort out his feelings. He wasn't so sure anymore that she didn't do both of them a favor by leaving. In fact, he was starting to question whether he was really in love with her.

He decided that he was really too tired to give it any more thought. He went to bed. As he stretched out on his bed, he found that his thoughts kept drifting back to Jerica. He was intrigued by the mystery that surrounded her. He wanted to know everything about her. She was the most mysterious woman he had ever met. He was anticipating their date Friday night.

Exhaustion finally took its toll and sleep came to Eric, but it was a troubled sleep, filled with dreams. He was dreaming of Jerica. She was standing in a large, vacant room. She was begging Justin to put the gun down, but he laughed and, aiming the gun, pulled the trigger.

Screaming "No!" Eric bolted straight up in bed. After looking around his bedroom, he realized it had been only a dream. But it had seemed so real.

Getting up, he went into the adjoining bathroom and splashed cold water on his face. The face that looked back at him from the bathroom mirror was one of dread and worry. He couldn't figure out why he had dreamed of Jerica and Justin like that. He didn't know either of them very well, but he could tell that they were very close. In fact, closer than most brothers and sisters were. Wiping his face with a towel, he couldn't shake the feeling that this had been more than a dream.

Sitting down on the side of the bed, he had the persistent urge to call her and see if she was all right. He couldn't, of course, but the urge was there. He was sure that she wouldn't appreciate a call at 2:45 in the morning. No matter how well intended it may be.

Besides, he had no sound basis for his feelings other than the dream he just had. *Why do I have this feeling of dread that something bad is going to happen to her? Why this great desire to protect her and from whom? Justin?* For an answer, he justified it by her beauty and the fact that he was totally taken by her. Besides, she was such an independent little thing he was sure she could take care of herself. She proved that the night he met her on the beach.

Someone must have really hurt her. Why else had she been on the beach? Suicide? No, she wasn't the type. She was in too much control of herself. She hadn't been

42

hysterical or distraught over finding herself in the position she had been in.

Whatever reasons, they were destined to meet, and he knew one thing—he intended to find out what the mystery was about her.

Once more sleep had eluded him, so donning his robe, he went to the kitchen. After rummaging around in the refrigerator, he decided to try a beer to see if it would relax him enough to sleep. The last thing he needed to do was show up at court looking like a zombie. He had to be at court at nine in the morning. He was trying a 4.8 million dollar case, and he needed to be as alert as possible. Besides, his father would not appreciate it if he did anything to jeopardize this case.

CHAPTER EIGHT

Eric was on his second cup of coffee when the telephone rang, startling him and causing him to spill coffee on his trousers. Cursing at his clumsiness, he picked up the telephone. "Hello?"

"Eric, its Dad. Our entire case has been blown apart! They found our key witness hanging in his cell this morning when they went to get him for court."

"What! Are you serious? That is just great. Are they calling it a suicide?"

"Of course they are. You and I both know better. They got to him. Somehow, they got to him. They had to have somebody on the inside. We had him locked up tighter than a drum. They knew that if he made it to the stand this morning, he would have destroyed them all. I've been all over this since I got the call this morning. I've demanded a full-scale investigation, but by the time we get anything, it will probably be too late."

Pouring himself another cup of coffee, he asked, "You're right, Dad, but what do we do now? Pierce was our star witness. Our only witness. Without him, we don't have much of a case against Dexter Pharmaceutical. It will be virtually impossible to prove their involvement in Pierce's drug dealings."

Eric could just see his father now, pacing back and forth the length of his office while they talked. "Maybe not. If we can get anything on that doctor, you know the one that was supplying him with the drugs... oh, you know, what's his name? Evans, Everin, Everette, yeah that's it. Everette. If we can come up with some solid proof that he was selling the stuff to punks like Pierce, we could nail them all. We are not out of the game yet. We still have some of those documents that Pierce provided us. I don't know what good they will do at this point, but at least it is something."

Blotting at the stain on his pants with a towel, Eric told his father that he would be in the office in about thirty minutes, and together they would see what they could do to salvage this case. In the meantime, his father was going to contact the DA and see if they had come up with anything on Pierce's death.

Hanging up the telephone, he threw the towel on the counter and went to change his pants. Going through his closet for the second time and still not finding his other pair of black slacks, he remembered that he had left them at the cleaners. Grabbing his tan slacks, he hurriedly changed.

Outside his building, morning was in full swing. For as long as he had lived in this building, the morning rituals of the other tenants hadn't changed. Somehow he found that oddly comforting to him.

Ms. McGurney was out on her routine walk with her toy poodle, Fifi. Mr. Flint sat on the porch talking to the birds. The birds actually seemed to understand him and talk back to him with their sing-song calls.

Eric stopped at Miller's newsstand to get a copy of the morning edition of the paper. He wanted to see what it had to say about Pierce's supposed suicide.

Eric decided to forego the subway in favor of walking to work so that he could enjoy the crisp morning air and warm, bright sunshine. He could not tolerate the crowded subway and all the rude, pushy commuters who frequently used it.

Fred, the doorman, greeted him with a cheery hello as he held open the door for him. Eric wished him a good day and headed for the bank of elevators that would take him up to his office on the 49th floor.

At the elevators, he encountered old Mr. Phipps, the janitor. For as long as he could remember, Mr. Phipps had been the janitor for this building. Even when he had been a child and his father used to bring him to the office with him, Mr. Phipps had been employed there. He always had a kind word for Eric, and today was no exception. "Good morning Mr. Hansen. You sure do look right smart in all your finery today."

"A good morning to you, Mr. Phipps, and I thank you. How are you doing on such a beautiful morning?"

"Son, I am just fine. I do hope you all done brought your umbrella with you. It's gonna come a gully washer soon."

Eric smiled at the old man. In all the years that he had been predicting the weather to Eric, he had never known him to be wrong. Of course, on a day such as this, when the sun was shining and the sky was clear and bright, it was hard to believe the old man, but believe him he did. "What time do you suppose it will start?"

After rubbing his hip and checking his watch he said, "I reckon it will start along about ten. You be ready for it now, ya hear?"

Eric assured him that he would be and that he had an umbrella in his office and then stepped into the elevator and pressed the button for his floor.

Exiting the elevator, Eric walked down the corridor to his office. He greeted his secretary and discussed the news with her about Pierce. He instructed her to hold all his calls and to tell his father that he had arrived and would come to his office in a few moments.

After a lengthy discussion with his father about their next move on Pierce's case, Eric engrossed himself in his notes. He was hoping to find some clue, even remote, to submit as evidence against Dexter Pharmaceutical and Dr. Everette.

Eric became aware of rain splattering against his windowpane. Checking his watch, he noted the time to be 10:02. "Mr. Phipps, you missed your calling. You should have been a weatherman. Even they aren't this accurate."

Smiling to himself, he thought if he had told anyone that it would be raining by ten that morning, they would have thought he was ready for a rubber room.

He was still smiling to himself when his secretary buzzed him to let him know that his new clients had arrived. He told her to give him a few minutes before sending them in. He reviewed his notes he had taken earlier this morning and quickly refreshed his memory.

Normally he did not accept clients over the telephone, but this couple had sounded so desperate, and since they had a court date in a week, his secretary had given them an appointment.

He buzzed his secretary to send them in. Standing to greet them, he was surprised to find himself facing a sweet, innocent looking elderly couple. He must have misunderstood his secretary. This couple could not possibly be accused of fraud.

After the introductions were out of the way, Eric got down to business. He found out that the Social Security Administration had accused them of fraud and had cut their benefits to less than half of what they had previously been receiving.

As it was, the couple was not legally married. They were living in a state of cohabitation, and as such, they could both draw their independent benefits. If they were married, their benefits would be combined, resulting in half of what they would draw independently, forcing them to live a meager existence.

After an hour-long conference, Eric assured them that he would do everything he possibly could to help them and get the charges dropped from their records. Eric told them not to worry and that he would be in touch.

He decided to call it quits for the day. Between the Pierce case and the fraud case, he was ready to relax. Grabbing his umbrella, he headed out the door to a good hard workout at the gym.

CHAPTER NINE

Jerica replaced the telephone in its cradle. Eric's secretary said that he could be reached at home. She had let the telephone ring several times before determining that he was not home and obviously did not have an answering machine.

Looking at her desk and satisfied that all was finished for the day, she turned out the lights, locked her office door, and left. She ran into a few of the girls from the office, and they invited her to come along and have a drink with them to unwind from the challenges that the day had held. She politely declined, explaining that Justin had been ill and she wanted to get home to check on him.

Arriving home, she found that Justin had obviously worked late. She made a casserole and put it in the oven. Taking up a novel that she had been trying to read for the past month, she curled up in her favorite chair. An hour had passed when the telephone rang. It was Justin letting her know that he was on his way home. He had made a major breakthrough on his vaccine and had stayed late to work on it. She told him she had a casserole in the oven and she would wait to eat with him.

After dinner, they watched a few television programs, then decided to call it a night. Jerica congratulated her brother on his vaccine progress then bade him good night.

Jerica's dreams were filled with visions of Eric. She dreamed of him holding her and kissing her. She woke up feeling warm and sensuous, only to be disappointed to find that it had only been a dream. The clock on the bedside table read 2:20 A.M. She fell back to sleep with thoughts of Eric and hopes that her dream would resume where it left off.

Morning found her preparing breakfast and yelling at her brother to get a move on or he would be late for work. He came into the kitchen as she handed him a cup of coffee and set his plate on the table.

"I thought I was going to have to drag your lazy bones out of bed this morning. I yelled for you about six times."

"I know. I heard you all six times. I was just getting a slow start this morning. I guess I'm not completely over that virus or whatever it was. I just needed a little extra rest."

"Are you up to going to work today?"

Smiling, her brother said, "You bet! I'm anxious to finish working on my project. I know that is it just a matter of time before I perfect it. I'm close. I can feel it!"

Jerica watched the enthusiasm play on her brother's face. He always did like solving the world's problems—and sometimes creating them. As a kid, he was always taking things apart and putting them back together again. He wanted to know what made things tick. It used to drive their parents crazy. Especially the time he had taken their mom's vacuum cleaner apart and failed to put it back together properly. It scared ten years off their mother's life when the thing started attacking her and tried to suck the dress off her back.

After that, she forbade Justin to take anything apart until she could find some "How To" books to help him restore the things back to their original form.

Justin told his sister that he would be late tonight and not to hold dinner for him.

"OK. Listen, I have to run. Have fun today, and win a Nobel Prize. I'll see you later tonight. Try not to work too hard. You still don't seem to be over those headaches yet."

Her brother heard the door shut and her car start. Getting up and stacking the dirty dishes in the sink, he too left the kitchen and prepared to leave for work.

On his way to work, he was listening to an oldies station. *It's My Party* by Leslie Gore was playing. He smiled to himself. That had always been a favorite of his sister's. Turning into the gate at work, he showed the security officer his identification badge. He pulled into his designated parking place. Grabbing his briefcase, he hurried to the lab, anxious to get started.

He was so engrossed in his work that he didn't hear the door open. When he looked up, the director and chief of staff were standing in front of him.

"I'm sorry gentlemen, I didn't hear you come in. What can I do for you?"

After sitting down, the director came right to the point. "I'm sorry, Justin, to bring this news to you so early in the day, but it couldn't wait. The financing that has been available for you to conduct your work has been pulled. It has nothing to do with you personally, you understand, I..."

"No!" Justin interrupted. "No, I don't understand. Why? They just can't pull money out from under you like that. We have commitments, agreements. What reasons are behind this?"

The chief of staff had been sitting quietly by up until now. Looking over at the director, he stood up. "Justin, this company is on the verge of bankruptcy. We are trying to cut back as much as possible on every level. We had to prioritize, and right now, this lab can be sacrificed. This lab is experimental work only. I know it is important work, but it's still experimental. This is something we can afford to do without right now." Spreading his hands out as if in apology he said, "It seems that someone has been dipping into the till. Of course, you will get six months' severance pay. I know that doesn't begin to compensate you for the loss of employment, and I apologize for that. I want you to know that if and when we get this company stabilized, you will be the first person we call back to work."

Justin sat in stunned silence. He couldn't believe what he was hearing. Laid off? Fired? When the realization hit him that he was actually being fired, only then could he find his voice to speak. "What about my projects? All my research and hard work? Because a few people messed up, everybody else is going to be punished?"

"Look, we know you are upset. We all are, but..." The director started out of his chair but was stopped by Justin's next words.

"Upset? Upset? Yes sir, I 'm upset! I'm angry! You're sitting there telling me that because someone got greedy and took a few bucks that I am out of a job! Are you trying to tell me that this company could not afford to lose a few dollars? How much did they lose? A few thousand?"

"Try two million dollars." The chief of staff got up and began pacing the length of the lab. "We don't know how this happened. We don't even know whom yet. We have a good idea, but we have no proof. Please try to understand. Our choices are very limited right now. Your check will be ready within the hour. Stop by my office, and I'll have it for you. I'm very sorry." With that, the men turned and left the lab.

Slashing out in anger at what was nearest to him, Justin swept the top of his filing cabinet clean in one sweep of his hand. He could not believe that nine years of research had ended all because of greed.

There wasn't any reason to stick around now. He went to the closet to retrieve some boxes and began emptying out his desk. After he left the lab, he drove around for awhile trying to sort things out. When he arrived home, it was a little after four that afternoon.

He stacked all his boxes in the garage for the time being. He couldn't imagine needing them for a while, if ever.

The phone was ringing as he walked into the house. Taking up the receiver, he was surprised to hear his sister's voice on the other end.

Jerica was expecting to get the answering machine and was surprised to hear her brother answer the telephone. "Hey, what are you doing home? I thought you were going to work late. You aren't ill again are you?"

"No, actually I'm unemployed."

Not believing what she heard, she asked him to explain. He told her the gist of it. She told him she had been planning on going out with some of her fellow workers but that she would come home instead. He told her to go ahead and go with them. He would prefer to be alone right now anyway. After assuring her brother that she would not be out late, she said goodbye.

After hanging up the telephone, she sat down at her desk. She was upset for him. He had always worked. When he was ten, he started mowing lawns and had worked ever since. Her brother was a workaholic. He thrived on work. She was not worried about him finding another job, but she was worried about his frame of mind. His research was so important to him.

Money had never been an issue. He would be fine if he didn't find another job right away. Their parents had left them a substantial trust fund. While she was contemplating what she had just learned, her secretary rang her to let her know that Mr. Jacoby was waiting for her. Grabbing her files and a pen, she hurried from her office.

Just as she stepped out of her office, Samantha stopped her and asked if she wanted to take a call from Eric. She knew she shouldn't keep Mr. Jacoby waiting, but the thrill of hearing from Eric was just too strong.

Grabbing the receiver, she answered, "Hello."

"Hi Jerica. I was just calling to make sure we were still on for Friday night?"

"Of course, unless you are trying to back out. Maybe you're having second thoughts about this boring dinner we're going to?"

Laughing, he said, "Absolutely not. Looking forward to it."

"Listen, I don't mean to rush or anything, but I'm late for a meeting with my boss. Call me tonight and we'll finalize our plans." Hanging up the telephone, she literally ran down the hall to her meeting.

***

Justin had been going through some of his work and sorting out which files he wanted to keep accessible when the front door opened and his sister staggered in. Taking one look at her, he knew she had more than her share to drink. His sister had never been a big drinker, and it was a rare occasion when she would get drunk.

"It looks like somebody had a good time. I hope you didn't drive home in this condition."

"No way, big brother. I am a resposti, respensil, no; I am a responsible drinker. I left my car at...somewhere, and one of the other girls who was the designated driver brought me home. I just hope I can find my car tomorrow." Laughing, she flopped down on the couch.

"Besides, it was happy hour, and at happy hour you buy a drink and get one free. I only bought four drinks. So that means I drinked, drunk, dranked—whatever—I had eight drinks. Which was actually seven drinks too many."

Laying his sister down on the couch, he put a pillow beneath her head and a blanket across her. Telling her to go to sleep, he stated that he would have something for her headache when she woke.

She tried to convince him that she didn't have a headache. While assuring her she would definitely have one in the morning, he watched her pass out. When she finally woke up, she was surprised it was midnight. Upon seeing his sister struggling to sit up, he brought her some tomato juice with an egg, some Tabasco sauce, and a dash of pepper. Stirring it up, he handed it to her, "Here, sis. Drink this straight down. It will make you feel better."

Sitting up and holding her head, she asked him what was in it. He told her she didn't want to know and to just drink it.

Doing as she was told, she made a horrible face when she handed him the empty glass back. "Justin Matthew Zimmerman! Don't you ever do that to me again! That was nasty."

Taking the glass out to the kitchen, he asked her if she wanted to rest a while longer or if she would she like to try eating a little something.

She told him she could probably keep something down. He came back carrying a tray with some cheese, crackers, and grapes.

As they ate, they discussed what had happened at the lab that morning. He told his sister that he had all day to think about this. Instead of letting it get him down, he was going to make the most of it. He was going to start by catching up on his much needed rest. Also, he would use the time to do some more research on her and find out why her body was able to rejuvenate itself the way it did.

After agreeing with her brother on his plans, she reminded him that he promised not to do any more tests on her.

CHAPTER TEN

The nightmares had started again. Justin had started having them when he was sixteen. The nightmares had lasted until he was about eighteen and then eventually tapered off until they were non-existent. Now they were back, along with the headaches, and he wanted to know why. Especially since they seemed to be more severe now.

He awoke with pain lashing at him. The nightmare he had was still vivid in his mind. It had seemed so real that he got out of bed and tiptoed to his sister's room to check on her.

Cracking the door open only enough to peer in, he was surprised to find her sitting up in bed. She was talking as if fully awake. Even as he watched her, she got out of bed and went to her dresser. She picked up her hairbrush and began brushing her hair. Then she calmly laid the brush down and got back in bed.

After making certain that she was safely in bed and back to sleep, he made his way to the bathroom to get some aspirin from the medicine cabinet. He decided that he needed something stronger, and after searching around for a couple of minutes, he finally found what he was looking for. Darvon was the only thing that seemed to give him total relief from these migraines. Shaking the last two tablets into the palm of his hand, he swallowed them down with a cup of water. He made a mental note to get his prescription refilled.

He had just finished rinsing his glass out and was heading back down the hall to his room when he heard his sister scream.

Running into her room, he found her sitting up in bed with the covers tucked tight around her chin, staring at the closet. Not sure if she was asleep or awake this time, he cautiously stepped into the room.

When she turned to look at him, he knew she was awake. He asked her what was wrong, and she said she really didn't know. She had a bad dream, and when she woke up, the closet was the center of her attention.

After searching the closet and assuring his sister that there wasn't anything in there to be afraid of, he double-checked the windows to make sure they were locked. Satisfied that all was safe and secure, he tucked his sister back into bed, and then, saying goodnight, he turned off her light and went to his room.

He was concerned for his sister. She had not had any nightmares since she was also sixteen. Now it seemed strange that after all these years, both were experiencing them again. He wondered what could be triggering them. Why now? He decided to talk with her about the nightmares and see if something was bothering her.

Lying down, he thought back to when they first had experienced the nightmares. He and his sister had shared similar nightmares. She would wake up screaming and holding her head, although she didn't have any pain, and he would wake up in a cold, clammy sweat with his head feeling as if it were going to burst.

They used to keep their aunt and uncle busy running from one bedroom to the other. Their aunt and uncle were wonderful people. They knew that the accident was the cause of these nightmares, and they would show love and patience to him and his sister on these occasions by holding them and letting them know that everything was going to be all right. They always sat with each child until they had gone back to sleep.

The doctors had assured them that, in time, they would cease to have the nightmares altogether. They had been right, of course. By the time they were in their teens, they had quit having them.

Tonight had been the third nightmare for him, and the first for Jerica in a long time. He couldn't help but think that he was forgetting something very important that would help him understand why these had started again. Something familiar was tugging at the edge of his subconscious, unable to make itself known.

He tried to analyze his dream. His sister had been falling. The rocks below were jagged and sharp. He knew that she was going to die, just as he knew she was going to live. Running to the edge of the cliff, he looked down. The body was lying there, broken and twisted. Looking into the face of the body, the glassy, lifeless eyes staring back at him were his own.

What did this mean? Why would he see his face looking back at him instead of his sister's? He decided that he was not going to get any answers tonight. His headache had abated enough to go to sleep. Pulling up the covers, he snuggled down and hoped to catch a few hours of sleep.

CHAPTER ELEVEN

Jerica was nervous about her date with Eric. This would be the first time she had seen him since they had gone to Pelican's Wharf for dinner. She was afraid he would be bored at this dinner party, but as it turned out, he knew as many people in attendance as she did.

She was impressed with the number of people with whom Eric was on first-name basis. Especially when she introduced him to Mr. Hoffmier and they greeted each other like old friends. Eric explained to her that he had represented Mr. Hoffmier in a couple of legal matters.

Admiring his modesty, Mr. Hoffmier informed her that Hansen and Hansen had been retained as legal counsel for his company for a number of years. This made Jerica realize how closely related her work was to Eric's.

Dinner was a pleasant affair. For appetizers, there were shrimp cocktails, followed by vishisquah, and a main course of pheasant under glass. The conversation that flowed around the table was comfortable and interesting. Her brother would have been totally uncomfortable this evening, whereas Eric was completely relaxed and in his element.

Upon leaving, Eric suggested they stop somewhere for coffee. They went to a little coffee shop known as Coffee, Bagels and More—the more being cappuccinos and specialty blends of coffees.

This was a place that was frequented by late night daters who hated to see the night end.

Eric and Jerica were no exception. During the course of the evening, they found they had much in common. Jerica had a passion for horses and loved to ride. She found herself telling him about the horse she had when she was fifteen. She had assured her parents, although she had never sat astride a horse before, that she was perfectly capable of riding a horse. Even after her parents ran to pick her up when the horse had thrown her, she assured them that it was a minor setback. In time, she had become a competent rider.

Arriving home, she invited him in for a nightcap. Her brother was still up, and the three of them passed the next hour in comfortable conversation. Justin told Eric a few childhood stories about his sister, with her countering with a few of her own about her brother.

Driving home Eric, marveled at the closeness that Jerica and Justin shared. As an only child, he never experienced that with a sibling. He envied them. In his apartment, he couldn't get Jerica off his mind. He had to admit he was more than just mildly attracted to her. He realized with a start that his feelings were more along the lines of love. He wondered if that could be possible. He had only known her for a short period. He didn't believe in the fairy tale of "love at first sight." Was such a thing possible? He decided not to look for an answer in that. Instead, he went to bed, and for the first time in weeks, went directly to sleep.

His dreams were of Jerica. They were lying in a field of purple flowers. He was lying on his back, looking up at a bright, clear blue sky. He was telling her how he felt. He rolled over to kiss her and screamed as blood flowed freely from a gash in her head. Drenched in a cold sweat, he bolted straight up in bed. The fear was still vivid in his mind as he switched on the lamp. Why did he keep having these horrible nightmares about her? Was this some kind of premonition? He didn't believe in them. He justified this by the way they had first met. Maybe subconsciously, he was trying to figure out why he found her lying at the edge of the water that night on the beach. That had to be it. There was nothing normal about finding a woman lying on the beach at three in the morning.

Whatever the reasons for his fears, he knew Jerica was beginning to mean something to him. Maybe that was the real problem. Maybe it was his fear of getting hurt by another female that was causing all this anxiety.

As he lay back down, sleep finally came to him. This time he slept dreamlessly.

Eric felt rested, refreshed, and ready to tackle another day. It was Saturday, and he had a few errands to run. He had to go shopping. He had to buy some groceries. There was nothing substantial in the refrigerator.

Reaching the market, he had to circle the parking lot two times until a vacant spot appeared. He almost gave up the idea of doing his shopping today. If it had not been for the fact that he was in desperate need of a few items, he would have run for his life.

The real nightmare began inside the market. There were people everywhere. One rather obese woman with five children trailing behind her kept blocking the aisles, making it virtually impossible for anyone to get around her.

Eric managed to avoid her until they reached the cereal aisle. If he hadn't wanted a box of shredded wheat, he would've given up the fight. But knowing how bad a cook he was, and not willing to be subjected to his own cooking, he bravely forged ahead. Finally securing the cereal without incident, he headed for the cashier's stand in hopes of beating the lady with all the children out of the store, only to have to stand in line for thirty minutes.

The cashier was a brassy, red headed, teenage girl who was wearing a mini skirt made out of denim and a low cut blouse tucked into the waistband of her skirt. Her hair was pulled up into a ponytail on one side of her head and her bangs were standing straight up from her forehead. This reminded Eric of an old banty rooster he used to chase around his grandparent's farmhouse when he visited as a child.

He was not at all surprised to hear the cashier announce his total in a shrill, whiny voice. Paying for his purchase, he declined the offer of having his bags taken to the car for him by one of the courtesy clerks.

Reaching his car, he found a note stuck under his windshield wiper. After reading it, he went to the passenger side. The whole side of the car from the front bumper to the middle of the door had a big, ugly scratch. Apparently, someone had a hard time parking in the slot next to his car. The note read, "Sorry, our fenders were attracted to each other." It was signed, "From someone who would never interfere with an attraction."

Cursing, Eric put his groceries in the car, and sliding behind the wheel, he muttered, "It was probably that fat lady with all the kids." Pulling out of the parking lot, he headed for home and made a mental note to call Jason's Garage to see if he could get his car into the shop next week.

At home, he stopped in the foyer to collect his mail. Depositing it in one of the sacks, he took the elevator up to the penthouse. Old lady Flannigan stopped him in the hallway to ask him if he had read the notice posted downstairs about the meeting that was going to be held Monday on the new rental regulations. He advised her that he hadn't but would make it a point to do so, foregoing the information that he owned his apartment and that the rental regulations didn't apply to him.

Letting himself in, he deposited the groceries on the table. Putting them away, he was interrupted by the telephone ringing. Crossing the living room, he picked it up on the third ring. "Hello?"

After the morning he had just spent at the market, the voice on the other end of the line was a welcome interruption.

"Hi Eric. I hope I'm not disturbing you. We talked about so much last night that we didn't decide on a time for you to pick me up. I was wanting to go visit with my aunt for awhile this afternoon and wanted to make sure I was back in town on time."

"You're right; we didn't. Will seven give you enough time?"

Thinking about the drive over and back, she said that would be fine. "What should I wear?"

Since they really had not decided where they were going, he said, "I guess that depends on what we are doing, huh? What do you feel like doing? Something fancy, or do you want to make it casual?"

"To be perfectly honest, after last night, casual sounds pretty good. Is that okay with you?"

"Sure, how about a movie? There is a really good film playing at the 71st Street Cinema."

"Sounds great." After a few more minutes of conversation, they hung up.

Eric was in a much better mood than he had been previously. Even the scratched fender was not as important as it had been earlier.

Finishing his groceries, he set about getting the rest of his errands done so he could concentrate on his date with Jerica.

CHAPTER TWELVE

The theater was dark and cool. Jerica was having a hard time concentrating on the movie. The light from the screen made Eric's face all that more attractive. She was so aware of him as he sat beside her. His cologne gave off a heady aroma. He rested his arm on the back of her chair and his thigh was pressed close to hers. She found herself remembering what it had been like when he had kissed her after their first date. What it had been like to be held in his strong arms. Those thoughts sent delicious shivers down her spine.

Eric, having felt her shivers, wanted to know if she was cold.

"No, I guess it was, you know, the old saying that somebody had walked across my grave."

Laughing, Eric said, "Yeah, my mother used to tell me that every time I did that, it was because I had a bad thought and it was trying to escape from me. To keep me a good little boy."

"Did you believe her?"

"Believe dear old mom? Of course, she wouldn't have told me an untruth. So just to be on the safe side, I never entertained another bad thought the rest of my life. That's why I turned out to be such a great guy." Grinning, he looked at her, and her heart fluttered.

"Yeah? Well the only bad thought I had was that I'm sitting here watching this fine feature film without any popcorn."

Laughing, he got up and said, "I get the message. I'll be right back. Plain or with butter? Never mind. I'll surprise you."

She watched him walk down the aisle. She liked the way he carried himself and the way his jeans hugged his hips. She found herself thinking that he was a magnificently built man and wondered what he would look like in a pair of swim trunks. She would just have to find out. Then she laughed to herself because here she was again thinking those "bad" thoughts.

After the movie, they stopped off at Caddy's for a drink. She had a frozen margarita and he had a Tom Collins. They spent the next hour talking. She told him about her work at Danforth and Jones, and he told her about his work as an attorney and what it was like to work with his father. He kept her entertained for the next hour with tales of the courtroom and some of the more comical aspects of being an attorney.

He told her about the time he forgot to wear his tie to court and the lady that he was representing loaned her sweater belt to him. It passed for one of the ties that the younger men were wearing today, but he was totally uncomfortable all during court.

Then there was the time that he was in closing arguments on a felony case and he was really trying to impress the jury. He went over to the table that held the water pitcher and glasses and was going to perch on the edge of it, when the whole table went crashing down. He ended up soaked completely through and had broken glass everywhere.

Instead of impressing the jury, they were recessed until the mess could be cleared away and he could obtain dry clothing.

His father thought he handled it rather well. Instead of being embarrassed by what had happened, he had simply stood up and announced to the room that his next trick would be to attempt to finish his closing arguments.

The jury had loved it. After the hearing was over one of the members of the jury came up and thanked him for giving them the only pleasant moment during the whole trial.

He related other cases that he and his father handled together. He had even admitted to her that there were a few times when he and his father had severely disagreed on certain cases. Jerica could tell that he admired his father a great deal. She appreciated a man that could be so open and honest about his relationship with his father.

She wanted to know more about him and his family. "So, tell me, what is your mother like? I picture her as a small woman with the strength of ten men and the absolute backbone of the family. I imagine both you and your father adore her."

With a rueful smile he said, "Yes, that was mom. She passed away right after I graduated from law school."

She was instantly sorry. "Oh Eric. I apologize. I didn't know. I didn't mean to bring up any bad memories. I just..."

"No, really it's all right. That was a long time ago, and as they say, time heals all wounds. You are right, she was a magnificent woman, petite, and the backbone of our family.

And Dad and I did adore her. Of course, my dad would never admit that she was the strength of our family. He is one of those men from the old school who think women have no strength except what they draw from their husbands. I believe there is truth in the old cliché, 'Behind every successful man is a good woman.' I know that is true in our case. My mom kept my dad going when he didn't think he was ever going to make it as a successful attorney. I know if it weren't for my mother, I wouldn't have become an attorney after watching my father struggle to build his practice.

"She made me feel as if I could do anything. She taught me that whatever I wanted I had to work for it and that nothing came free. She said the challenges and struggles that I had to endure to achieve my goals would help build my character. She was right.

"Her strength gave me the ambition to continue to strive and to succeed. Because of that, even after her death, I knew that no matter what I did, it would have made my mother proud, and that is something I will never forget."

She was touched by what Eric had just shared with her. She was sure that he had showed emotions to her that he didn't usually share very easily.

"At least you knew what she expected of you, and she had a chance to see part of her dream for you realized before she died. Don't ever be sad about that."

The sad look that crept into her eyes pulled at his heartstrings. He wanted to know what had put it there. "Why the sudden sadness?"

"I was just thinking about my own mother. She passed away when I was sixteen. My father, too."

Eric was surprised. For some reason, he had assumed that her parents were still living. "Now it is my turn to say I'm sorry. Want to talk about it?"

"There isn't much to talk about really. We were on vacation. The first one my parents had been able to, or willing to, take in six years. We were going to Disneyland. We were driving in the mountains and were rounding a curve, and a drunk driver was in our lane. We were hit head on. Our car traveled about twenty-five feet down a ravine. We were all thrown from the car. My father and mother were killed instantly.

"My brother and I were in bad shape. Justin sustained two broken legs, some internal injuries, and a fractured vertebra. At the time, the doctor's didn't think he would ever walk again, but my brother, being the strong willed type, told them they were wrong. And he set out to prove it to them.

"Even when we were kids, he never gave up on something he wanted or believed in. It was something a little short of a miracle that he finally did start walking again. It took a year of surgeries and many months of therapy before he took his first step. The doctors were amazed. They had given up on him because of the damage, but he knew he could do it. Since Justin believed he could do it, I believed he could do it. Now except for a slight limp that, is hardly noticeable except on cold, rainy days which makes it more defined and causes him a little pain, you can't even tell he ever had a problem."

Moved by the circumstances surrounding her life, he was curious about how she came out of the accident.

"At first I was unconscious. When I came to, I saw my parents. I knew that they hadn't survived. I saw my brother and tried to go to him but wasn't able to. I couldn't move. The funny thing, though, was that I didn't feel any pain. To this day, I still can't explain that.

The paramedics finally arrived, and after looking at my parents, they knew they couldn't help them, so they started attending to my brother. He kept yelling at them to take care of me. They told him they needed to attend to him first. They thought I was dead. He kept yelling at them that I wasn't dead and to please help me. I tried to yell at them to tell them that I wasn't dead, but I couldn't get my voice to cooperate. I guess one of the attendants finally heard me because he turned around and looked at me. He ran over to me, and the next thing I remember is waking up in the hospital. They told me that I had been pinned under the car. One of the wheels had been resting partially on my head. They couldn't figure out how I had survived.

"After I was released from the hospital, I had to go back for some therapy. I had suffered some memory loss. I could remember the accident and the fact that we had lost our parents, but I couldn't remember anything up to that point about my life. I was in therapy for about sixteen months, then it all finally started coming back to me.

"They gave me my walking papers, and now, with the exception of an occasional migraine or nightmare, I am fine. In fact, those are the only problems Justin and I seem to have. Otherwise, we are healthy. Justin's headaches are more severe than mine are, and he has them more frequently than I do. Now, let's change the subject to more pleasant matters."

CHAPTER THIRTEEN

Eric and Jerica found that they had a good many things in common. Except for a few brief moments after she had told him about the accident, their conversation had flowed freely.

He was in the middle of telling her something when he stopped and got very quiet. Looking up to see what had gotten his attention, she saw that he was looking across the room. What she saw was a most attractive woman sitting with an equally attractive man. "Do you know them?"

Pulling himself together, he looked at her and answered, "Yes. Up until about ten days ago, we were engaged to be married."

Surprised, she turned to look at the woman again. "I'm sorry. What happened? Did you love her a lot?"

"At the time I thought I did."

It was at that moment that the woman turned, and, upon seeing them, paled slightly. Rising from their chairs, they made their way over to Eric and Jerica's table. Scowling, Eric said, "I was hoping to avoid having to speak to her, but naturally she would come over here. If for nothing but simple curiosity as to your identity."

When the couple arrived at the table, Jerica turned to face a very attractive woman. Eric introduced her as Donna Reynolds. In turn, she introduced her escort as Beau Tollbridge. With the introductions out of the way, and out of obligatory politeness, Eric asked if they wanted to join them for a drink. Oblivious to the tension that this meeting had sparked, Beau accepted the offer for them.

Jerica was uncomfortable for Eric. She could tell this meeting had unsettled him. Donna, having recovered, appeared comfortable as they placed their drink orders.

After a few brief minutes of discussing the weather, the conversation changed to something of a more relaxed nature. Beau was interested in what Eric did for a living. "I believe Donna said you were an attorney. What kind of law do you practice?"

"Actually, we do a little bit of everything, but we specialize in criminal."

The conversation had eased the tension and was going well. They talked about everyone's jobs and interests. Then Beau said something that shattered the moment.

"I have a bit of good news. I have finally gotten Donna to agree to tie the knot with me. I have been begging her for the past nine months. We have been dating for the past fourteen months, but I knew right from the start that she was the woman for me. After all my groveling, she finally said yes."

Eric's anger was apparent as he made their excuses to leave. As he helped Jerica with her chair, he said his good byes. Walking out of the restaurant, he left a very bewildered Beau and a wide-eyed Donna behind.

In the car, Eric was visibly shaken. She wanted to console him, but not knowing how, she decided it would be better to remain silent.

After a lengthy silence, he apologized for his behavior, and pulling into a Homeland parking lot, he offered her an explanation.

He told her that Donna had broken off their engagement the very night he had found her on the beach. In fact, she had been the reason he had been out there to begin with. He could not figure out why she had broken it off without much of an explanation. Now things were finally coming together. The missed lunches. The broken dates. The telephone calls that were never returned. Here he had been blaming himself because he had no other explanation, only to find out that it was her all along. He was relieved to know why. It hurt his pride that she had been seeing Beau at the same time, but at least he now knew. He finally had closure. He could move on.

Grabbing Jerica, he hugged her. She didn't know the reason behind it and was not about to question it. She was right where she had been longing to be. The hug turned into more of a caress, and she found herself melting into his arms. When his lips demanded hers, she gave them willingly.

Lost in the ecstasy that engulfed them, they were both startled when a flashlight beam hit them. Rolling down his window, he looked into the face of the officer. "Sorry to disturb you folks, but aren't you a little to old to be parking? Especially here?"

Laughing, Eric stepped out of the car and explained to the officer why they were there. As the two men walked towards the squad car, she saw Eric take out his billfold and present his license to the officer. She hoped the officer wasn't going to give them a ticket.

A few moments later, they walked back to the car. The officer told them to enjoy the rest of the evening, and winking at her, he got into his car and left. They realized how they must have looked to the officer. They both burst out laughing.

Deciding that they had enough excitement for one night, he drove her home. They sat in her driveway talking for a few minutes. Eric pulled her into his arms, and, kissing her tenderly, he asked her to go on a picnic with him the next day. She agreed, and after another kiss, she told him good night and got out of the car. He walked her to the porch, kissed her again, and left.

As she kicked her shoes off inside the door, Charlie came running to her to be let out. Picking him up and giving him a big hug, she asked, "Charlie my boy, what would you say if I told you that I think I'm falling in love?"

Completely startled, she jumped when a voice answered, "I think I would say that love is one of the greatest emotions two people can share, and from the look on your face, I would have to agree that you are."

She looked up at her brother, "What a sneaky thing to do. Why didn't you let me know that you were still up and standing there?"

"What? And miss seeing that look on your face? No way. I wouldn't have missed that for the world. If you ask my opinion, which you didn't, but if you did, I would have to say it's definitely love. Yeah, it's love."

Knowing her brother wasn't going to let up on her, she threw one of her shoes at him. Ducking, he asked her how her date went.

She told him about running into Donna, Eric's ex-fiancée, and about the effect it had on Eric. Then she told him about the officer catching them in the parking lot. Yawning and stretching, she told her brother that she was tired and ready for bed.

They locked up and headed down the hall to their rooms. Opening her bedroom door, she heard her brother say, "I certainly hope it is love, sis. I certainly do."

CHAPTER FOURTEEN

Morning dawned bright and the day promised to be clear and beautiful. Rising from the bed, Jerica slipped on her housecoat and slippers. Making her way to the kitchen, she heard Charlie at the door demanding to be let in. As she bent over to pick him up, the telephone rang. Putting him back down, she went to answer it before the ringing woke up her brother.

Hearing her Aunt Kat's voice on the other end of the line panicked her. She said that they had taken Uncle Jack to the emergency room this morning. They were not sure, but it looked like he could have suffered a stroke. "Please come! I'm so frightened! I need you and Justin with me."

Assuring her aunt that they were on their way, she went down the hall to awaken her brother. She almost collided with him in the hallway, and he could tell by the look on her face that something was wrong.

After explaining the call from their aunt, they both ran to their rooms to get ready to go. Reaching in her closet for her shirt, she remembered that she was supposed to have a picnic date with Eric. She knew she should call him and let him know what was going on. Dialing his number, she wasn't at all surprised that she woke him up. The hour was still early for a Saturday.

"Eric, this is Jerica. I'm sorry to call you so early, but an emergency has come up." She explained to him about her uncle.

"Of course, I understand. Is there anything I can do?"

Thanking him for his concern, she told him that she needed to hurry but that she would call him and let him know something as soon as she could. Hurrying down the hall, she yelled for her brother to hurry. They didn't know how long they might need to stay at their aunt's, so they decided to pack enough clothing for a few days. If she needed anything else, she would worry about it later.

After she closed and latched her suitcase, Justin stepped into the room, took it from her, and went to load the car.

Locking the door and making sure that Charlie had enough food and water for a few days left inside the garage, they were ready to go.

"Did you let Charlie out?"

"Are you kidding? The minute I opened the back door, he was history. I guess he knew we needed him to cooperate this morning." Turning to her brother, she said, "Let's go."

The drive was a little short of three hours. If they didn't stop along the way, she figured they would arrive about ten-thirty or so if the traffic was with them.

On the drive to the hospital, they discussed the possibilities of Uncle Jack's survival. They both knew he wasn't getting any younger. He was in his late sixties, and Aunt Kat was not far behind him. They knew that if anything happened to him, they would have to help Aunt Kat.

Their aunt and uncle had a unique relationship. They weren't merely just husband and wife; they were best friends. They had been married for over forty years and spent every day together since both were retired.

Justin decided they needed a quick break. They stopped at a truck stop to get something cold to drink and to use the restroom. Since they had missed breakfast, they decided to grab something quick to eat. The traffic had been light, and they were making good time. They had a little over an hour's drive ahead of them. They could still make it to the hospital by eleven. They might not get another chance to eat for quite some time.

They ate quickly, then jumped back in the car and headed out. They knew their uncle was in good hands with Dr. Daily. He had been their aunt and uncle's family physician for the past thirty-five years.

Justin broke the silence. "I love that old man. I don't think I could handle it if anything happens to him. He has been as much a father to me as our own dad had been."

She knew how close they were. She and Aunt Kat were just as close. Fate had stepped in and robbed their aunt and uncle of their own children on whom to bestow their abundance of love. Therefore, in return, they had lavished all their love on Justin and Jerica. They had made a very close knit family. Anyone who had not personally known them couldn't tell that they weren't their real parents.

"Don't worry. Uncle Jack is a strong man. He has always been in good condition. I'm sure he is going to be fine. Besides, Aunt Kat said they weren't sure what was wrong. They only thought it was a stroke. Let's be positive here." Reaching over, she took her brother's hand.

Arriving at the hospital, they stopped to ask directions to their uncle's room. After being told that their uncle was in the intensive care unit, the nurse directed them to it.

After making several turns down the hospital corridors, they came upon their aunt. She was sitting in a chair looking small and lost. Gingerly approaching her, Jerica said, "Aunt Kat. We're here."

Looking up, she flew into her niece's arms. "Oh Jerica, I'm so glad you're here." Hugging her tightly, she turned and pulled Justin into the embrace. "Thank you for coming. Let's sit down and I'll fill you in on what's going on."

Taking their aunt's hand, they led her to the chair she had occupied minutes before. Jerica sat next to her, and her brother took the chair on the opposite side.

"The doctor said that he had a heart attack. Can you believe it? He has never been sick a day in his life. I can't understand it. They have been running tests on him all morning. He didn't seem to have any symptoms leading up to this. The doctor said that usually there are symptoms. Your uncle didn't complain about anything. He didn't seem to feel badly. If he was having any trouble, he didn't say anything to me."

She broke down and started to cry. Taking his aunt into his arms, Justin assured her that he was going to be okay. He was getting the best medical attention possible.

The hours passed slowly as they waited to see how Uncle Jack was doing. Justin and Jerica took turns going for drinks and coffee. They tried to entice their aunt to eat but she refused, saying she wasn't hungry.

It was late in the evening when the doctor finally had some news for them. Instantly they were on their feet when they saw him approaching. Demanding to be told everything, Aunt Kat said, "Don't lie to me, Fred. We've known each other too long for that. I want to know exactly what is going on and what to expect." .

Sitting her back down on the sofa, he explained to them what had caused their uncle's heart attack. "Half of the main artery at the back of his heart has been blocked off, cutting off his blood supply. Sometimes when this happens in other arteries, the heart can draw blood from different sources, but in this case, it couldn't. Did he say anything to you about chest pain? Had he been feeling bad lately?"

"No, he seemed a little tired, but he didn't say anything about any pain. He has been sleeping more than usual the past couple of days. Fred, if he was having any trouble, he kept it from me because he didn't say a word."

"Well, it is possible he didn't know he was having trouble. Most people do know it though. Did he ever get cold and clammy feeling and comment about it?"

"No, but the other day when we were working in the yard, I did notice that when he was bending over and stood up, he seemed to make a terrible face. When I asked him what was wrong, he said it was probably gas. He was sweating pretty heavy though."

The doctor took her hands as a gesture of comfort. "Katrina, you and I both know how strong Jack is. Sometimes these things just happen without any warning signs. Some people experience what is called 'angina'; others get no warnings at all, or warnings that aren't aware of. All we can do now is wait. The next forty-eight hours will be critical. If he can hold his own for that period of time, then I think we have a chance. We will need to do some surgery to get that artery opened, but he is not strong enough right now. Once he has stabilized, then we can take care of that.

Right now, I suggest that the three of you go home and get some rest. There isn't anything you can do here. If there is even the slightest change in his condition, good or bad, I will call you. I'm staying here at the hospital. Kids, take your aunt home."

Kissing Aunt Kat on the cheek, the doctor went back towards Uncle Jack's room. Taking his aunt by the arm, Justin said, "Come on, Aunt Kat. You heard the doctor, and he is right. Let's go home. You need some rest."

All the way home, their aunt complained that she should have stayed at the hospital. Once they were home, she still refused to settle down for the night. She went into the kitchen and began to prepare some food. Any time their aunt was upset, she would cook or bake something. It kept her busy and her mind occupied, so they just left her alone.

Justin had been in the garage, and when he came in, he knew his aunt had baked an apple pie. His taste buds had immediately reacted to the smell. His aunt made the best apple pie around. Coming up behind her, he gently planted a kiss on her cheek. She turned and gave him a tremulous smile.

Jerica walked into the kitchen just as the telephone rang. Three pairs of eyes flew to the telephone hanging on the kitchen wall. Justin grabbed the receiver; he motioned that it was the doctor. After a brief conversation, he replaced the telephone back on the hook. Turning to the other two, he told them Uncle Jack had taken a turn for the worse and they needed to go to the hospital.

In complete control now, Aunt Kat ordered them to get ready. Turning to the stove, she turned it off and, without looking back, went to retrieve her purse. No one spoke on the way to the hospital. Each was silently praying to God for help for their uncle's recovery.

The doctor met them at the nurse's desk. He took Aunt Kat down to Uncle Jack's room while Jerica and Justin waited. After about fifteen minutes, she returned. Her face was pale and she was visibly shaken. They didn't think he would make it through the night. The doctor wanted her to call whomever she needed. The family minister was the only other person who needed to be notified.

The doctor allowed each one in to see him for five minutes. Afterwards, he took them to his office. He explained to them what had happened and what to expect. He hated having to tell them this. This was something he had to deal with every day, and it never got any easier, especially when it was close friends like this.

He had been with Jack and Kat when they had gone to pick Justin and Jerica up from the airport. He had seen to all their childhood accidents and diseases. He watched these two grow up and move away.

"My friends, I have done everything humanly possible and used all the modern medicines available. Now it is in God's hands." With that, he quietly left the room, giving them time to deal with their emotions.

CHAPTER FIFTEEN

Jerica watched as the sun came up over the tops of the trees that lined the parking lot. Uncle Jack had made it through the night. The doctor had allowed Aunt Kat to sit with him for awhile. She had peeked in to make sure that both were all right and found her aunt talking to her uncle although he was unconscious. She told him how much she loved him and that it wouldn't be fair for him to leave her now in their golden years when they had so much to look forward to.

Quietly shutting the door and giving her aunt her privacy, she went to find her brother. He was just stepping off the elevator with two cups of steaming coffee. Gratefully, she took one from him and told him what she had overheard. He commented that it did not hurt anything and who knows, it might even help since it had never been proven if people could actually hear when they were like that or not.

Another hour passed before their aunt joined them. She was feeling better and her hopes were renewed. She had been talking to Uncle Jack and telling him about what was going on. While she had been talking to him, he had squeezed her hand. It was just a slight pressure, but she knew he had heard her. The doctor said it could have been a reflex motion, but she knew it wasn't. It was her husband's way of telling her that he was going to be okay.

At a little past noon, the doctor came out and told them that he had regained consciousness and was asking for them. The doctor warned them not to let him talk much and to stay only a few minutes.

Entering his room, they found him smiling wanly. Jerica and Justin kissed their Uncle Jack then moved out of the way for their aunt. After she kissed her husband, he told her he was going to be just fine.

By evening, he had improved greatly. He was even able to sit up for a few minutes at a time. They even allowed him a little chicken broth for dinner. After visiting hours were over, they left for home.

Jerica prepared a simple meal while Justin took the apple pie out of the oven. It had finished cooking to a golden brown and was delicious.

Jerica excused herself and went to telephone Eric. She had promised to call him as soon as she could and felt bad that she had not been able to. She knew he would understand. They spent several minutes on the telephone and before hanging up, Eric made her to promise to call back as soon as she could.

Turning around, she came face to face with her brother, "Wipe that stupid grin off your face! You look like a big baboon, and stop following me around and listening in on my calls."

As she threw a pillow at her brother, he laughed and said, "Now I know why they call these 'throw pillows.'"

They filled their aunt in on who Eric was, but left out the part on how they met. They knew she would not understand let alone approve.

Aunt Kat was glad Jerica had found someone. "He sounds very nice, and I would like to meet him sometime. I'll be old, gray and dead before your brother ever finds someone to settle down with and make me a grandma."

Justin looked at his aunt with a devilish grin and said, "How do you know I haven't already made you a grandma?"

"Justin Matthew Zimmerman! You better be joking or I'll get the hickory stick to your backside. Why don't you go out in the garage and find something to do? We have women talk to discuss."

Laughing, he left the room. Upon hearing the garage door shut, Kat turned to Jerica and said, "Okay, tell me everything. How did you meet him?"

Leaving out many of the details, she told her aunt they met at the beach. Of course, she did not tell her that he tripped over her lying in the water, or that it was three o'clock in the morning. She told her that they had a couple of dates already and were planning on another one.

Kat could tell that this man was very special to her niece. She had never seen her this way, and it made her happy to know that finally she had found someone special.

Waving a white flag in the door, Justin asked if it was safe to come back in. They passed another hour of companionable conversation and decided to call it a night and get some rest. They wanted to go to the hospital early the next day.

After all the lights were out, Jerica found herself unable to sleep. Eric's voice kept running through her mind. She found herself fantasizing about him. She was in Eric's arms. His breath was warm against her cheek. She turned to look into his eyes, and what she saw there took her breath away. He kissed her. His lips demanding as hers eagerly responded.

Realizing this train of thought was never going to let her sleep, she decided to get something to drink. She tiptoed into the kitchen. She rummaged around in the refrigerator and came up with a wine cooler. Hoping it would relax her enough to go to sleep, she sat down at the kitchen table to drink it.

After finishing it off, she went back upstairs, climbed into bed, and pulled the covers up under her chin. In a little bit the wine had done the trick, and she began to doze off. She never had been able to hold her liquor.

CHAPTER SIXTEEN

The surgery had gone well, and by the end of the week, Uncle Jack was well on his way to recovery. He was going to have to take it easy for awhile, and his diet was going to be restricted, but other than that, he was going to be fine.

Jerica and Justin loaded the car and prepared to leave for home. Jerica knew she was going to have to play catch up at work for the time that she had missed, which would result in overtime at the office. She decided to go to the office on Saturday. That way she would be able to get some things done without the normal interruptions of a regular workweek, and hopefully by Monday, she would be back on track.

They arrived at home around eight that evening. Charlie was sitting on the front porch waiting expectantly for them. When they stepped out of the car, he started meowing and didn't quit until they had unloaded their bags and were inside the house.

Jerica scooped him up in her arms. Normally Charlie wouldn't allow anyone to hold him for any length of time, but he had missed her enough to allow himself to be held briefly. Jumping from her arms, he ran to the kitchen and let her know that he was hungry. She opened him a can of food and he attacked it with vigor.

Justin came in with the mail, while his sister played back their recorder to see who had called in their absence. She was pleased to hear that Eric had called four times.

After unpacking, she went to the telephone to call him. Picking up on the first ring, he was hoping desperately that it was Jerica. At the sound of her voice, the tension of the past few days began to leave him.

They spent several minutes in conversation while she told him about her uncle. Eric knew that if he didn't see her soon, he would go crazy. "How about that picnic tomorrow? You owe me one."

She wanted desperately to say yes, but she knew she really needed to go to the office. Instead, she said, "I can't. I need to go to work tomorrow and see if I can catch up on some of the work I've missed. How about a rain check?"

Eric, hearing the hesitancy in her voice, played on that. "Oh, come on. Tomorrow is Saturday. No one should have to work on Saturday. You deserve this. You had a rough week. Take the day off, relax, and tackle everything on Monday. Come on, what do you say?"

She had to admit his reasoning was good even if his motives weren't. She found herself agreeing to go with him, and after making final plans, they said good night.

Eric whistled a tune as he prepared the things they would need for the picnic. Making a list of things to do, he wrote down a stop at the liquor store for a bottle of wine. Flipping off the kitchen light, he went to take a long, relaxing shower.

His thoughts kept straying to Jerica. He found himself wanting to be with her every moment. To be able to kiss and hold her. He realized that even Donna had not produced these kinds of feelings from him, and it made him wonder at how Jerica could have captured his attention without really trying. In fact, he had been the aggressive one in this strange relationship. He couldn't keep from calling her, using any ruse to see her.

With Donna, it had been just the opposite. She had chased him from the start. They had met at a dinner party given by one of his colleagues. From the moment she was introduced to him, she had been a constant companion by his side the rest of the night. All night long, she had made none too subtle hints at where the night could end if he was willing. Once, he had a chance to sneak outside for some fresh air and she had found him. They ended up going to her house for a nightcap, and he left the next morning. Never during their two-year romance did he ever feel like he was in control of their relationship.

Unlike Donna, Jerica had been an absolute lady while in his company. She was kind and considerate. Not once had she ever hinted that their relationship could be any more than what they were sharing now. He found it strangely comforting to know that when he was with her, he was not expected to be anything but himself.

Donna had demanded they go to every social event. She had to be seen. To be noticed. He found that Jerica liked just being with him. They didn't have to go anywhere or do anything. She was as comfortable in blue jeans as she was in a dinner dress and was adaptable to any situation.

Drying himself off, he finally admitted that she had gotten to him. He turned in early that night. He wanted everything to be perfect for their picnic tomorrow. Drifting off to sleep, he envisioned her face. He slept with a smile.

CHAPTER SEVENTEEN

The weather promised to be perfect for a picnic. Dressed and ready to go, Eric grabbed the picnic basket. Just as he was going out the door, the telephone rang. "No way! Not today, telephone. I've got plans to spend the entire day with a beautiful woman and no one is going to stop me. So ring all you want." Pushing the elevator button, he stepped inside.

On the elevator he crowded in between the rather large lady who lived on the sixth floor and the man who worked for the city refuse department. Sandwiched between the two of them, he wasn't sure if he would make it off the elevator alive. As the door opened, he was the first one out. Greeting the doorman with a cheery hello, he ran to his car.

They found the perfect place to eat. It was a plush, secluded, shady area next to a running stream. Eric helped Jerica spread out the blanket. Together they set the food out of the basket. The menu included fried chicken, potato salad, baked beans, coleslaw, cheese wedges, grapes, and a nice bottle of Beringer wine.

Wanting to contribute to the lunch, Jerica had brought a delicious, homemade pineapple upside down cake. Eric let her know that was his favorite cake and joked that they should just go straight to the dessert first.

Their hunger sated, they decided to walk along the water's edge. Jerica couldn't resist the urge to feel the cold water on her feet, so stripping her shoes and socks off, she stepped into the water. The coldness sent little shocks of delight throughout her body.

Laughing at her look of surprise, he explained to her that the stream was spring fed. It was that cold all year around.

Deciding that he needed to join her, she splashed him and took off across the creek. Needing no more prompting than that, Eric shed his shoes and socks, and took off after her.

Looking behind her, she yelled when she realized he was closing in. She ran harder, but she was caught off guard when the water became a little deeper and she plunged face first into it. Sitting up and sputtering, she looked up at Eric, who was standing over her laughing.

"Are you okay? Did you hurt anything?"

Looking at him she said, "Only my pride. Look at me. Be a gentleman and help me up."

Reaching to help her, he was surprised to find himself pulled down beside her. Laughing, he began to splash her. Calling it a truce, she said she had enough and was going to get out.

Climbing out of the water, she looked down only to find her blouse had become transparent. Embarrassed, she crossed her arms over her breasts but not before Eric had noticed.

The sight sent Eric's blood racing. Not able to keep himself in restraint, he pulled her to him and kissed her with all the passion he was feeling.

They moved together with a hunger that neither of them had ever experienced before. Thrusting his tongue deep inside her mouth, he tasted her sweetness. A sigh escaped from her as Eric lowered her down onto the blanket. Offering no resistance, they embraced as passion flared.

Sitting up, she said, "Eric, don't. Someone might see us."

"No, this is a very private creek. I know the owner personally, and there isn't anyone near for fifty acres in any direction."

"How can you be so sure?

Smiling at her, "I own this land." He took her lips in his again and they let the passion consume them.

Struggling to regain control, she pushed him away. Blushing, she had to admit to him that she was still a virgin. She was saving herself for her wedding day.

She was surprised when Eric pulled her to her feet. He told her that he admired her for that and respected her decision. Wrapping the blanket about her shoulders, they spent the next couple of hours talking and enjoying each other's company.

It was at this moment that she knew she was sitting here enjoying the company of the man she was going to marry. With that thought in her mind, she smiled lovingly at him as they packed the basket to go home.

Upon Jerica and Justin's insistence, Eric stayed for dinner. They decided to grill some steaks out on the patio.

There was a deep friendship developing among the three of them as they prepared dinner together. Justin could tell that his sister and Eric were developing strong feelings for each other, and he liked that idea. He could tell by the way that they looked at each other and the little touches and shared smiles between them.

He was sure his sister was in love and felt certain that Eric felt the same way. His sister had dated other guys, but never had he seen such a glow of happiness on her face as he did now.

The rest of the evening the three of them spent talking and laughing. Justin decided to call it an early night, using the excuse that he needed to get up early. His sister, of course, knew this was just an excuse to give them some time alone. Her brother was no longer employed and didn't have to be up early.

Meeting her brother's eyes, she saw him wink at her. Blowing him a good night kiss, he pretended to catch it and went into the house.

Lounging on the recliners while sharing a glass of wine, they contemplated the expanse of the universe and how wonderfully made it was. They both agreed God had indeed given mere mankind something so wonderful to enjoy, as well as something useful.

It was a little past one when Eric finally left. Jerica went to take a long, hot, relaxing bath. She met her brother coming down the hall.

"Did Eric leave?"

"Yes, he has to get up early. He's playing golf with his father. They are teeing off at 7:00. I'm going to take a bath, then hit the bed." Kissing her brother on the cheek she said, "Thanks bro."

"What for?"

"You know what for. For giving us time together."

Grinning at her he said, "I think he will make a nice addition to the family."

Laughing at him, she closed the bathroom door, and he could hear her singing softly to herself.

Jerica was up early the next morning. She had a mountain of household chores that needed to be done before she could think of going to work on Monday. She put a load of laundry in the wash, mopped the kitchen floor, dusted, and swept the entire house.

Bending over the bathtub to scrub it, she heard her brother come in the door.

"Stay off my kitchen floor! I just mopped it."

Finding his sister bent over the tub, Justin asked, "How long before it is dry? I'm starving."

"About a half hour or so."

He complained that he would starve while waiting for the floor to dry. Having a passion for pizza, he enticed her into going with him to the Pizza House. She told him to give her a few minutes to clean up and they could go.

At the Pizza House they ordered an extra large pizza with everything on it. Her brother's appetite never ceased to amaze her. She did well to eat two pieces of pizza while he devoured the rest of it.

On the way home, they stopped off at the store for some more cleaning items she needed. Her brother teased her that since she started dating Eric the house had never been so clean.

"OK brother. Since you seem to have a problem with me doing all this house cleaning, I have a job for you. When we get home, you get the privilege of cleaning your bedroom. I was in there trying to find the dirty laundry, and I couldn't tell what was clean and what was dirty. Not to mention the overall filth that is starting to trickle out into the hallway."

Laughing at his sister's description of his room, he said, "Okay, you're right. It is about time to do something with it."

They worked together the rest of the afternoon both cleaning and repairing until they fell exhausted into their chairs in the living room. Neither of them had the energy to cook dinner, which was just as well because they decided they were too tired to eat.

It was a welcome gesture when Eric called offering to bring in Chinese. Suddenly their appetites returned, and accepting the offer, they set about getting ready for his visit.

The three of them sat around talking, laughing, and eating until they couldn't take another bite. Justin reminded them that they had fortune cookies to eat. Since they were too full to eat them, they decided to read their fortunes anyway. Cracking open a fortune cookie, Jerica read, "You are destined to love deeply and be loved deeply in return." Looking over at Eric, she felt her fortune was indeed coming true.

Justin opened his and reading it to himself, he laughed. His sister asked him what it said. "Beware of hidden dangers." He told them he had run into that problem while cleaning his room that afternoon.

Eric's was the strangest of the three: "You will be the key to unlock the secret of death."

Everyone laughed. but it left Eric with the strangest feeling that this was a warning of some kind, a premonition. To cover his apprehension he was sure was apparent on his face, he tossed his on the table and said, "I can just see who writes this stuff. A bunch of fat little oriental men, sitting around a poker table in a smoke filled room, cigars or cigarettes dangling from their lips. Each determined to outdo the other on who can come up with the silliest fortunes."

CHAPTER NINETEEN

Monday morning was everything Jerica expected and more. The top of her desk was buried beneath a pile of papers, and her message board was full. Her secretary was in the middle of a crisis with her computer and the telephone had been ringing off the wall non-stop since 7:30.

Telling her to take care of her computer, she grabbed the telephone. A dissatisfied client went into detail telling her about his accounts while she juggled paperwork on her desk.

She assured the man that everything would be taken care of and she would get back in touch with him as soon as she had a chance to pull his file and see what was going on.

Instantly the telephone rang again, and snapping it up, she barked, "Hello."

Hearing the tone of her voice the caller said, "I'm sorry, I've called at a bad time."

Immediately recognizing Eric's voice, she apologized to him. She told him how her morning was going already and that she was a little short on patience.

He assured her that it was ok. He understood. "I know you're busy, so I won't keep you. I wanted to see if you wanted to have dinner with me tonight. Nothing fancy. I figured you would have a rough day and wouldn't feel like going home and cooking."

"Eric, that is very sweet of you, but I would need to fix dinner for Justin anyway."

"No you don't. I already talked to him and he agreed to meet us for dinner."

"Oh, ganging up on me are you? Okay, where and when?"

"I'll pick you up about 5:15 in front of your building. Your brother told me that your car is in the shop. Now it's settled, get back to work. I'll see you later."

Talking to him had put her in a better mood. She began to tackle her work with a better attitude.

About three that afternoon things began to settle down. She looked up to find her secretary standing at her office door with two steaming cups of coffee.

Grateful for the interruption, she bade her secretary sit down. Taking the cup of coffee from her, she let out a long sigh as the warmth spread through her. "Thanks, I didn't realized how badly I needed this. This has been one heck of a day hasn't it? I'm sorry you had so much put on you with me being gone last week."

"Yes, it has been a rough day, but all in all, we managed to get everything done. We make a good team, boss lady. I think in regards to the day you just spent, you should be convinced of how important you are to this company. You were only gone a week, and this place almost came to a stand still. I was afraid we were going to have to shut the doors."

Smiling at her secretary's loyalty, she said, "Well, I'm sure it wasn't that bad, but thank you for the support anyway." The telephone ringing brought moans of protest from both women. Motioning her secretary to stay where she was, Jerica reached for the telephone.

It was the janitor wanting to know if she would rather have hunter green paint instead of the canary yellow in the secretaries' lounge. She told him to go with the hunter green.

As she replaced the receiver, they both laughed. "I believe that is the easiest decision I have had to make all day."

The next couple of hours passed by quickly without any major incidents. After clearing her desk and making sure nothing was left unfinished, she left the building to meet Eric.

True to his word, he arrived at precisely 5:15. Stepping into the car, she leaned over and kissed him.

The restaurant they went to was a favorite place of hers. Her brother was waiting for them in the anteroom. Upon giving Eric's name, they were directed to a table. Justin placed a kiss on his sister's cheek and asked how her day went.

"If you want to have a pleasant dinner, I won't answer that question just now."

Laughing, he said, "Okay, how is that pretty secretary of yours then?"

After telling him that her secretary was just fine and thanks for asking, they changed the subject to more pleasant matters.

The meal was delicious. Eric felt as if he was sharing dinner with his family. Being an only child, he never had the chance to know a relationship such as these two enjoyed. He felt privileged to be a part of this. It was at that moment he knew for certain that he was in love with Jerica. He just wished he knew exactly how she felt.

Although Justin had assured Eric that his feelings were reciprocated, he wanted to hear it from her.

As they left the restaurant, Justin asked Eric to drive his sister home because he had to go to the library.

Arriving at home, they met a very hungry and demanding Charlie on the front porch. As she was trying to open the door, Charlie kept running in and out of her legs, then darting in just as the door was opened.

Jerica filled his bowls with milk and some of his favorite cat food then left him to eat. Walking back into the living room, she went straight into Eric's arms.

Turning her to look at him, he said, "I love you Jerica. I think I have from the first moment I saw you."

She couldn't believe what she just heard. He loved her! She had wanted to voice the same thing to him but had been afraid that he wouldn't feel the same way. Grabbing him and hugging him, she breathed, "I love you too, Eric."

Basking in their newfound love, they talked of a future together. They agreed that they should take it one day at a time. She knew from his experience with Donna that she would have to win his trust completely.

They were talking about their dreams and ambitions when her brother came through the front door. Glowing, they told him how they felt about each other and asked for his blessings.

"So you two finally figured it out. I wondered how much longer it was going to take you."

It was getting late, and Eric made ready to leave. After he told Justin good night, he and Jerica walked out on the front porch.

They spent another couple of minutes together, then he kissed her and left.

Going through the house, she locked up and turned the lights off, then went to bed. As she was drifting off to sleep, she vowed to be all that Eric would ever want in a woman.

She awoke feeling refreshed and ready to tackle another day. She new she had a mound of work waiting for her today, and she was ready.

Yelling at her brother to get a move on or he wouldn't get any breakfast, she went to the kitchen to get started.

He came into the kitchen rubbing sleep from his eyes. "Since when did you become drill sergeant?" Taking a cup from the cabinet, he poured himself a cup of coffee. Sitting down at the table, he reached for the sugar bowl.

Cracking eggs in the skillet, she asked him, "What's the matter, grumpy? Didn't you get enough sleep?"

Yawning he said, "Actually, I didn't. I think I'm trying to get another headache."

Concerned, she looked at her brother. He did look a little pale this morning. "Justin, why don't you go ahead and call Doc Fletcher? He might be able to help you before that thing gets too painful."

"No, he'll tell me the same thing he always tells me. Take your medicine; rest as much as possible, no reading. You know the story. I'll be okay. I took my medicine about two hours ago, and I'll rest for awhile this morning."

"Okay, but take care of yourself. If you need me for anything, call me at work." She placed his breakfast in front of him and was worried when he didn't do much but pick at it.

Noticing his sister's look of concern, he forced himself to eat a little bit just to keep her happy. "Sis, I was wondering, I've been doing some research on you. I think I have come up with some interesting material that might be pertinent to your situation. I was thinking that if we did one more test that I could..."

"No, Justin! No! You promised me, no more tests. This isn't open for discussion. We agreed not to do this anymore, didn't we?"

"Yes we did. You're right. I'm sorry sis."

Kissing her brother goodbye, she left for work.

He was still sitting at the kitchen table thinking about another test after she left. He felt certain that the accident had been the cause of his sister's unusual circumstances. From the research he had done, it seemed that something within the brain itself was altered as a result of the pressure from the wheel sitting on her head for so long a period of time.

What was happening to his sister was unique. There had been a similar occurrence in South Africa. A man was unloading cargo from a merchant ship. He was under the hoist, directing the operator on where to unload the cargo, when the cable snapped, dropping the entire load, approximately 850 pounds, on him. He had sustained some minor injuries that healed nicely when he should have been killed. The only difference there was between this person and his sister was that he only lived for five years after that accident. Justin had contacted his twin brother and had been told about all the accidents that his brother had experienced up until the last one that had taken his life.

His brother couldn't give Justin any more information than that because they never did figure out how he could have survived the things that happened to him either.

Jerica's accident had been twelve years ago, and she seemed to only be getting stronger with each accident, or "tests," as he called them.

Getting up and refilling his coffee cup, he went to retrieve his notebook. He had a plan forming in his mind. A new test was beginning to take shape. He thought to himself, *If Jerica knew what I was thinking she would turn tail and run. However, I have to know what this is all about. I need to know how my sister can survive death.*

Sitting down with a fresh cup of coffee, his thoughts began to travel back in time. He was remembering the first test and the events that led up to it. He remembered what the outcome had been and that his sister had been fine afterwards.

It was at that time in his young life that he knew he was destined to be a scientist and uncover the secrets of the world. He had a need to fulfill. He needed to know why his sister had the unique ability to preserve her life.

CHAPTER TWENTY

Justin asked his sister to go to the movies with him. It was Friday night, and she didn't have any plans with Eric, so she agreed to go.

He suggested they stop for a cold drink on the way to the drive in. Jerica saw some of her friends there and went to talk to them while they were waiting on their order.

The carhop brought their drinks. Making sure that no one was watching, Justin dumped a packet of white powder into his sister's drink. Stirring it with the straw, he made sure that none of the powder was visible. Then he took it to his sister.

Handing her the cup, she took a long drink. He watched her for any signs that she might be able to taste the drug. She didn't seem to notice.

Not knowing how long it would be before it took affect, he suggested they leave in time to make it to the theater.

It wasn't long before she told him that she was feeling funny. Looking at her brother, she asked him, "Did you put something in my drink? You promised! Why are you doing this to me?" After that, she passed out.

The stuff he had given her was very potent. He had told the clerk at the feed store that he needed the most potent of poisons available. He said he had a rat infestation and needed to kill them out in one swipe.

The clerk had assured him that this would do the trick, and it only took a small amount. He could put it out in powder form or he could put it in food. Since it didn't have a taste or smell to it, the rats would go for it quicker in food. He told him to be careful and keep it away from people because it didn't take much to kill a person, and to be sure to wash his hands when he was through spreading it around.

Assuring him that he would be careful, he went home and hid the poison in his room. He had to wait until the time was right to use it, and the time had come about two weeks later.

Justin took Jerica to an old abandoned house that he had run across while rabbit hunting one time before. Taking a blanket, lantern, and camera out of the trunk of his car, he went inside and spread the blanket out, lit the lantern, and got the camcorder ready.

Carefully laying his sister down on the blanket, he checked the camera to make sure it was ready to tape. He turned it on and sat down to wait.

She was lying with her arm under her head, her glassy eyes staring sightlessly at her brother.

Saying a prayer, he focused the camera and took two pictures of his sister. Closing her eyes, he checked for a pulse and heart beat and found none.

Taking up his notebook, he made some notes. Leaning back against the wall he prayed, "Dear God, please let me be right. If I'm not this time, please forgive me and take my sister to Your heart."

The camcorder was the only sound in the room as it documented everything that was going on. Justin sat patiently waiting, watching, and occasionally taking his sister's pulse and heart beat only to find none.

He didn't have to wait as long as he expected to. About two and a half-hours later, he detected a slight pulse and heart beat. Making notes on his book, he kept a close watch on his sister.

Moaning, his sister struggled to sit up and looked around. Seeing her brother, she asked him what had happened.

Looking at his watch, he made some more notes in his book, and saying a prayer of thanks, he looked at his sister and smiled. "Hi. How do you feel?"

"I guess that would depend on what you did to me. Where are we and what in the world did you put in my drink? My mouth tastes horrible!"

He answered her questions, then asked, "What is the last thing you remember?"

"We stopped for a cold drink. I talked with some friends. We got in the car to go to the movies, and then I remembered feeling sick and dizzy. That's it. I can't believe you did this! You promised me you wouldn't do this again. Why, Justin? Why did you break your promise to me? When is this going to stop? When I am finally dead?"

He knew she was very angry with him so he tried to console her. "Come on, sis, don't be mad at me. I took this test because I think I have found the answer. I did this one a little different than the last ones. Always before. we assumed you were dead but never really had actual proof. I mean, sure, I threw you in the water unconscious, but I didn't stay to see if you really were dead. I wasn't sure you drowned. You could have come to and swam to shore, because I made sure we were close enough. Now I have proof, and I got it on tape.

"Justin, we both know that I was dead. Why was it necessary for this test?"

"Remember the accident? The ambulance attendant even thought you were dead. He didn't actually take your pulse or anything. He just assumed you were dead. You were trapped under the wheel of the car. You told me you wanted to tell us you were alive, but you couldn't get the words out. Why? You said you could hear him talking but you couldn't make him hear you. I saw you. No one should have been able to survive with a car sitting on his or her head like that but you did. The only evidence to show that you were even in that wreck is a small hairline scar. Something happened. Something so bizarre that can't be explained. We need some answer, sis. Don't you want to know?"

"Why do we need some answers? Why can't we just live with this? We have no logical explanations, no proof that I was actually dead in the wreck. I know that since then you have done numerous tests, but you just said yourself that you never stuck around to see if I was actually dead. We have no proof!"

"We do now. I got all this on tape. Now I can study it, and maybe there will be an answer for us. I checked your pulse and heartbeat several times while you were lying there. You didn't have one for almost three hours from the time I gave you the rat poisoning until you came to. Look at these pictures I took of you."

When he handed her the Polaroids he took of her, she was shocked to see her own lifeless face staring back at her. Her mouth hung slack and white foam ran from one corner of it. Leaning back against the wall, she realized that her brother was right. Here was the proof they had needed. She had indeed been dead. Handing the pictures back to her brother, she said, "Now what? Where do we go from here?"

Unable to hide his excitement, "I don't know. I need to do some more research. Maybe with this tape and pictures I can come up with some logical explanation. I should have done this a long time ago, and maybe then we would finally have answers. This is great! Just think, sis, you cheated old man death.... Again."

They spent the next several hours in that old shack discussing the possibilities, and coming up empty handed, they finally gathered their belongings and took off for home.

They both agreed they would never tell anyone what they had discovered. They knew that if they did, Jerica would have no moment of peace. Her life would no longer be her own. She would be made into a human guinea pig. Making a pact, just as they did when they had been children, they promised to keep the secret just between them for life or longer.

Making a joke, her brother said, "In your case, keeping this secret for life could really be forever."

Throwing her brother a look, she said, "You could be right. Besides, who would believe this anyway? I don't believe it myself. And I know it is true!"

CHAPTER TWENTY-ONE

Glancing around the kitchen, Justin realized that he had been sitting there for an hour. Getting up, he gathered the dirty dishes and put them in the dishwasher. He hated Mondays. He always had but even more now that he was unemployed. He figured he had better find something to do or he would go stir crazy.

Climbing the ladder to the attic, he searched around until he found all the files he had kept on his sister over the years. He found all his boxes of notes, except one. That was the box he needed the most. It had the notes he made the first year they discovered her unique gift.

For hours, he poured over his notes. He was starting to see a pattern take shape. Each test, with the exception of the most recent one, had taken progressively longer, but this last test had been shorter.

He wondered if the nature of the test or the way death had occurred in each case was a factor in the length of time. He got out a column pad and listed each test, the nature of death, the time of death, the time she returned, and the particular instrument of death used. He kept thinking there was something right in front of him that he was missing. The answers remained elusive.

Rubbing his head, he felt another headache coming on. Going to the bathroom, he rummaged around in the medicine cabinet until he found what he was looking for. He took a couple of aspirin. Then he went to fix himself a light snack. Taking his plate into the living room, he turned on the television. He finally found a channel that didn't have a daytime soap opera or a game show on it.

Two hours later the program ended, and he got up to take his dirty plate to the kitchen. Taking some steaks out of the freezer, he placed them in the bottom of the refrigerator to thaw for dinner. He promised his sister that he would put them on about five o'clock. He prepared the potatoes for baking, turned the oven on, and slid them in.

Dinner was ready and on the table when his sister walked through the door. She had missed lunch and was starving. She complimented her brother on the steaks. He had cooked hers just right.

Together they cleaned the kitchen. Justin approached the subject of the test. "I was wondering if you remember all the tests that we have tried on you?"

"I was wondering when you were going to bring that up. Besides, what do you mean we, rabbit? I believe that should be you have tried on me. I haven't had a whole lot to say in the matter. Anyway, you have to be kidding. It is not everyday a girl is murdered by her brother and lives to talk about it. Right?"

Going for his notebook, he sat down next to her. "Look at these notes. I have been trying to figure out if there is a pattern to these tests, if there is a common element. So far, I haven't come up with anything because each test has been different. I was thinking that if you read these notes then maybe you would come up with something that I might have missed. I feel that the answer is staring me in the face, but I can't see it."

Agreeing to read them, she reminded her brother that he was the scientific one. "I don't know what good it will do, but I'll read through them. I don't even know what to look for."

"Anything. Anything that looks different or might make sense to you, or, for that matter, anything that does not make sense, since we really don't know what we are looking for anyway."

Taking the notebook from him, she asked him if this was the only one she had to read or if he wanted her to read everything he had. He told her she needed to read everything.

"Just start with this one first. I've outlined each test, the cause of death, and the elements involved, time frames, things like that. Feel free to make notes out to the side if you want. In fact, use a red pen so we can read them later."

Skeptical, she looked at her brother. "Okay, I'll try, but don't expect too much from me." Taking the notebook, she asked her brother to put on a fresh pot of coffee because it looked like a long night.

She was so engrossed in her reading that she did not hear her brother calling to her. He came in from the garage and told her to get the telephone; it had been ringing for some time.

It was Eric. He was finding it extremely difficult to stay away from her. They spent the next forty-five minutes talking. After hanging up, she was pleased that she would be seeing him on Friday.

Picking up the notebook, she resumed reading. She was amazed as some of the things her brother had actually done to her. She was so engrossed in her reading she didn't realize it had gotten so late until she looked at her watch.

Tossing the notebook aside, she went to the kitchen to get a fresh cup of coffee. Her brother stepped in from the garage, covered from head to toe in dust. He told her that he didn't find the other box he needed and said he would look again tomorrow. He headed for the shower while his sister headed for bed. She had to be at the office early in the morning. She couldn't believe she had stayed up this late reading.

Blowing her brother a kiss good night, she went to her room. A few minutes later she heard the shower running.

CHAPTER TWENTY-TWO

The week went by quickly, and Friday night finally arrived. Jerica was preparing for her date when her brother knocked on her bedroom door. After telling him to come in, she went back to fixing her hair.

Justin stood just inside the door, leaning on it and watching her, grinning like the cat that ate the canary.

"Okay, hot shot. What are you up to?"

Still grinning, he told his sister he finally found the missing box.

"I searched from one end of the attic to the next. You know where I found it? It was in that trunk of Mom and Dad's. The one that was locked and we never found the key to. Aunt Kat must have put it in there when we moved out. I decided to try the lock, and it just snapped open. Weird, huh? Anyway, the box was sitting there right on top. I don't know what else there is in that trunk, but you might want to look at it later. I brought it down and stuck it by the back door in the garage."

She couldn't believe it. They had tried several times to get that lock open without breaking it. Aunt Kat said she didn't have a key to it and seemed rather vague as to the contents of the trunk. It probably only held some old papers of their parents', but if that was the case, then why did their aunt seem so reluctant to talk about it? Maybe it had been too hard for her to deal with after their deaths. After all, it had been her only sister killed in that car wreck.

Eric greeted Jerica with a kiss. He looked great. He was dressed in a black suit with a light green shirt. He looked so handsome that he took her breath away.

After a few minutes of small talk they left for the restaurant.

They made a striking couple as they entered the restaurant. The maitre d' showed them to their table. Neither of them spoke until he had taken their wine order and went to retrieve it. Eric had told him to bring a bottle of his best champagne because they were celebrating.

Looking at him questioningly, she asked him what they were celebrating. She thought that maybe he had won his case for the elderly couple, who had been accused of fraud from the Social Security Administration. He told her he did, but that was not what they were celebrating.

Raising his glass in a toast, he said, "To us. Never has there been a more suited couple. We are destined to share a unique and wonderful love. Thank you for loving me and letting me love you."

With tears in her eyes, she raised her glass to his and vowed her love to him and they drank deeply. The she said, "Okay, my turn. To you, Eric. For being the man of my dreams. For making my life more meaningful by loving me and teaching me how to love you in return. And for allowing me to be everything you want in a woman."

Eric drank to her toast, then setting the glasses aside, he reached across the table and kissed her. With all the love he felt shining in his eyes, he said, "I can't even really begin to tell you what a difference you have made in my life. I only hope that you will continue to love me as much as I love you.

I know what we have is very special. I felt it from the first moment I laid eyes on you. I love you, Jerica."

Just then, the waiter interrupted them to ask for their orders. They chatted pleasantly throughout the meal. Both felt content in the knowledge that they loved each other. Even when they had the misfortune of running into Donna and Beau again, their mood didn't change. They refused to let anyone or anything ruin their evening.

It unnerved Donna to see Eric so happy in his relationship with Jerica. She had hoped he was still distraught over their break up. She found that she was missing him and that Beau was not all what she had hoped he would be. She had made the wrong choice in men and wondered if there was a chance she could get Eric back.

Donna made blatant overtures to Eric while they chatted, and finally a very angry and hurt Beau ushered them out of the restaurant.

Jerica was annoyed at Donna's obnoxious and blatant behavior. She was pleased that Eric had found her behavior as repulsive as she had.

"I can't believe she acted that way. She acted no better than a common streetwalker. I can't blame Beau for being angry. If she had done that to me, I would have strangled her right here. He showed more restraint than I would have.

"I can't believe I ever thought I was in love with her. Well, let's not let her ruin our evening. Where were we? Oh, yeah, I believe we were right about here." Leaning over, he kissed her, and this time it was uninterrupted.

Coming around to her side of the table, he helped her from her chair and they left the restaurant. They encountered Donna and Beau in the parking lot having a horrible argument. They nodded in their direction and hurried to the car to avoid having to have any confrontation with them.

After helping Jerica in the car, Eric hurried around to his side and jumped in. Just as he was getting ready to pull out, Donna looked up at him at that moment and waived her arms to get his attention. He put the car in gear and ignored her. They didn't want to get into the middle of a lovers' quarrel.

Jerica looked back just as Donna tossed her evening bag on the ground while Beau drove off leaving her standing there. Laughing, she turned around in her seat. "I hope Donna has enough money for a taxi because Beau just left her standing there."

Neither of them wanted the evening to end, so they went back to Eric's apartment for a nightcap. They sat side by side talking and holding hands. Eric pulled her into his arms, and their kisses belied the desire they both were trying hard to keep in control.

Pulling away from him, Jerica whispered, "Eric, you make me feel so wonderful. I never knew that love could be so good between two people. If I had known that a man and a woman could share so many wonderful things, I would have fallen in love a long time ago."

Looking deep into her eyes, he said he was glad she hadn't. "If you had fallen in love before this, then I wouldn't be here now. You can't begin to know the feelings you inspire in me. I feel more confident about myself. I feel special enough in your heart that you want to share your life with me." Kissing her, he knew that if he didn't take her home soon, he would compromise everything that they had come to mean to each other.

It was getting harder and harder to control their desires. They joked that maybe they should hire a chaperone for them when they went out together. He assured her since he would be a gentleman, one wouldn't be needed.

On the ride back to Jerica's, they made plans to have breakfast together the next morning. She wanted to cook for him. They planned breakfast for eight at his apartment. She said she would bring what she needed with her in case he didn't have it on hand.

Laughing, he said that was a good idea since he never shopped for major groceries.

Kissing her good night, he said he would see her later.

CHAPTER TWENTY-THREE

Jerica arrived early the next morning to prepare breakfast. She was very efficient in the kitchen, and Eric was greatly impressed with her culinary talents. He found enjoyment watching her work around the kitchen, and it pleased him to think that some day soon he would always be able to watch her prepare breakfast.

Donna hadn't been the domestic type. She hated the idea of cooking and made no attempt at it at all. She would have gladly pampered herself with breakfast out, therefore avoiding not only the cooking but the cleaning up as well.

Taking a bite of gravy, Eric rolled his eyes. He had never tasted anything as delicious as this gravy. "Where did you learn to make such wonderful gravy? This stuff is great!"

Smiling at him, Jerica replied, "I learned it from my Aunt Kat. It is an old family secret recipe. If you're a good boy, maybe someday I'll share the secret with you."

"Well, even if you shared your treasured secret with me, it wouldn't do any good. I couldn't even begin to make it taste as good as this. My only attempt at making gravy ended up with me creating the super ball."

Laughing, she looked at him.

"No, really. Don't laugh. I'll tell you the story behind it. I used to watch my mom make gravy, and it always looked easy. So one day, I guess I was about twenty-three and in college, I got hungry for some of my mother's gravy. I decided since she wasn't here to make it for me, I could do it since I had seen her do it so many times before.

"I did everything I remembered seeing her do, and I was watering at the mouth to eat. It started getting thick and looked delicious. I kept stirring as I had seen my mother do, and it kept getting thicker. I guess I realized there was a problem when it got to the point where I could no longer stir it, and my spoon was stuck right in the middle of the pan. So, I let it cool for a little while, then I scooped up a spoon full and rolled it into a ball, and it bounced all over my kitchen. I rolled up several more and did the same thing. If I had only known what I was creating, I could have been rich. Oh well, some other poor gravy-hungry slob came along and invented the super ball."

Jerica was laughing so hard tears were streaming down her face. Holding her sides, she begged him to stop so she could catch her breath. Eric proceeded to tell her other humorous stories of his college days. He liked the sound of her laughter and he wanted to keep hearing it. They spent the next hour telling each other funny stories trying to outdo one another.

Jerica finally gave up. She knew that no matter what story she told, she couldn't win. He just led too exciting a life. Compared to his life, hers had been boring. The only exciting thing she ever experienced was the strange and unique phenomenon of her body recovering from death. She wondered what he would think about that. He would probably think she was crazy. Would she blame him? If the circumstances were reversed and he told her a story like that, she wouldn't believe it either.

Deciding not to say anything to him, she found herself surprised that she wanted to confide in him at all. Their relationship was still too new, although they both knew how they felt for each other.

At two that afternoon she decided to go home. She had a few things that needed to be done today. One of those things was to go through that old trunk. She had been looking forward to doing that since her brother had gotten it open last night. She was curious as to what wonderful treasures of her parents were hidden away in that old trunk.

Reluctantly, Eric let her leave. He decided since he couldn't talk her into staying with him the rest of the day, he might as well go to the office and catch up on some work. He could get quite a bit done without any interruptions.

He mused to himself that before Jerica had come into his life, that was how he had spent every Saturday and didn't mind doing it. Now he found it a rather tedious task that he needed to do. Not even Donna had been able to keep him from going to the office on Saturday. He used the excuse that Saturdays were his most productive day without the daily interruptions. Now he realized that was exactly what it had been...an excuse.

After spending several unproductive hours, during which most of his time was spent thinking about Jerica, he decided to call it quits. Picking up the telephone, he dialed her number. The sound of her voice sent delicious thrills throughout his body, and then he realized he had gotten her answering machine. Leaving her a message to call him at home, he turned off the lights, locked the door, and headed home to a very lonely apartment.

CHAPTER TWENTY-FOUR

Jerica had heard the telephone ringing but was so astounded by what she had discovered in the old trunk that she had let the machine answer it. She didn't feel like talking to anyone right now.

Taking the stack of papers with her, she went in search of her brother. She found him descending the attic stairs as she stepped out the garage door.

"Hey, what's wrong? You look like you've seen a ghost."

"Justin, come inside a minute. I've got something you need to see." Sitting down at the kitchen table with him, she placed the papers in front of him and told him to read them.

After several minutes passed, he looked up, "Where did you get these?"

"They were in the trunk. What do you think this means? Do you think Aunt Kat and Uncle Jack know about these?"

He couldn't believe what he was looking at. "They must have known. Maybe that is why a key could never be produced. Maybe they were trying to keep this from us."

"But why? What does all this mean?"

"Maybe Aunt Kat was trying to protect us from the contents of this trunk. She always seemed uneasy when I questioned her about it. I think it's time we get some answers."

Shuffling through the papers again, he asked her, "Do you realize that these papers could be the answers we have been looking for? I can't believe this. How can this be?"

Laying the four papers out on the table he looked from one to the other. The first one was a birth certificate for an infant girl. She was born October 1, 1960. The name on the certificate was Jerica Dawn Zimmerman. The second paper was her brother's birth certificate with his information on it.

The third document was a death certificate for an infant girl. Age four months old. Cause of death was bronchial pneumonia and it was dated, February 12, 1961 at 4:07 p.m. The child listed on it was Jerica Dawn Zimmerman.

The fourth paper was another birth certificate for an infant girl. It was dated February 12, 1961, at 5:49 p.m. This also was for Jerica Dawn Zimmerman.

Justin's excitement was beginning to grow, "Jerica, don't you realize what this means? It means the accident didn't cause this. You've been doing this since birth!"

She was stunned as she looked at the papers. "I can't believe this. If this is true, then Mom and Dad knew about this all along. Aunt Kat and Uncle Jack must know about it as well. Why didn't they ever tell us? Aunt Kat had to have put your notes in here deliberately. She must have known about the tests. Why didn't she say something then? Why all the secrecy?"

"I don't know, but I think you and I need to take a little trip to Aunt Kat and Uncle Jack's and get some answers."

She agreed with her brother, and they made preparations to leave that evening. Jerica called her Aunt to let her know they were coming down but didn't say why. Then she called Eric and told him they had to leave again for a few days. She told him they just wanted to go check on Uncle Jack's condition.

Eric could tell she was upset about something and made her promise to call him as soon as she could to let him know she was all right.

"I love you Jerica. Have a safe trip and call soon."

"I love you too. I'll be in touch." Hanging up the telephone, she went to her room to pack. She yelled at her brother to put Charlie out and put enough food and water down for him for a few days.

They left town determined to get the answers they had been searching for.

CHAPTER TWENTY-FIVE

Aunt Kat met them at the door as they turned in to the driveway. She had been watching for them. She could tell by the urgency in Jerica's voice that they knew. She had dreaded this day and always knew the possibility of their finding out was there. She knew that one day she would have to face them on this, and today was the day. She still wasn't prepared even after twenty-eight years.

Embracing each of them in a hug, she escorted them into the living room and went to prepare them some tea. Setting the tray down on the coffee table, she poured each one a cup.

Satisfied that they were both comfortable, she began. "I knew curiosity would eventually win out, and you would eventually figure out how to open that trunk. If I had listened to my heart and thrown those papers away years ago, you wouldn't be sitting here now, and I wouldn't have to tell you what I am about to tell you."

Standing up, she said she was going to go get Uncle Jack and then they would talk about it.

Their aunt and uncle returned from the garage and sat down on the sofa. Kat began, "We promised your parents that unless you asked, we would never volunteer this information. They only wanted to protect you children. Maybe we shouldn't have kept it a secret. We don't know. Many a time we discussed this. We knew that Justin's curiosity was going to get the better of him and well, I guess it has."

Getting up, she began to pace the living room. She stopped and turned to face them. "Jerica, you were the most beautiful baby girl I ever saw. There was not a more beautiful child in the world, except for you, Justin. Since you both looked alike, it was hard to say which was more beautiful. Your parents were so proud of the two of you. Everything they did in life was for the benefit of you children. They doted on your every need. You were special babies from day one. Your parents had tried for years to get pregnant, and just when they had given up hope of ever having children, you came along.

"As you know, your parents had you late in life. Your mother underwent countless operations to help her conceive. They tried every method known to man and every drug that was available back then. Your mother even went to a herbalist doctor she knew in Africa."

She sat down and took Jerica's hand. "Your mother had a very difficult pregnancy. When she was six months along, she became very ill. The doctors never really knew what was the matter with her. They thought it might have been a rare strain of flu brought in by the military from overseas. Your mother was in intensive care for a little over two weeks. She lost so much weight that they were afraid she was going to miscarry. You could hardly tell she was pregnant. Being pregnant in those days, you could not take any drugs. She wasn't able to get the medicine she needed to get rid of the flue or whatever disease she had. The doctors didn't think she was going to make it. They wanted to terminate the pregnancy to give your mother a fighting chance to live, but she refused. They were afraid that if she did manage to carry to term, there could possibly be some birth defects.

"Your mother had two major setbacks during those two weeks. Her heart quit once and we really thought we had lost her. The second time, her kidneys started acting up but the doctors were determined to keep her alive. That, along with your mother's determination to live, paid off.

"She finally reached a stage when we knew she was going to make it. She was still very weak and had to remain in bed for the duration of her pregnancy. But in the end the birth went better than expected."

They knew this story was difficult for their aunt and uncle to relate. It was bringing back some sad memories for all of them.

"Aunt Kat, what has all of this got to do with the papers we found in the trunk? Why do I have two birth certificates and a death certificate?"

Taking a jagged breath, Kat continued the story. "Your parents finally recuperated from all the disasters they had been experiencing. Your mother got healthy again. Then Jerica, you took sick. Your parents thought it was just a cold, but they couldn't get you well. You became listless, wouldn't eat, and started losing weight. They did everything they could and finally they took you to the hospital.

"They pronounced you dead on arrival and your parents were absolutely devastated. They said it was bronchial pneumonia, but they really weren't sure what it was.

"The coroner officially pronounced you dead on February 12, 1961 at 4:07 PM. Then they took your little body away to the hospital morgue."

Aunt Kat swiped at the tears that streamed down her cheek, while Uncle Jack gently rubbed her arm. Jerica squeezed her aunt's hand and it seemed to give her the strength to continue her story. "It was somewhere around 5:30 or so that evening that we asked to see you one last time. Your parents had been taken to another part of the hospital where they had sedated your mother.

"Your Uncle Jack and I stood by that table looking down at you. We couldn't believe that you were brought into this world only to be taken away from us like that. There had to be a mistake. You looked like a little angel lying there asleep. I took your little hands in mine and they were so cold. I remember rubbing them, as if somehow I could rub some warmth back into them. Your uncle was holding Justin and he was crying for you. It was as if he knew that you were gone and never coming back. Your uncle finally had to take him out into the hall to calm him down. While I was standing there, the doctor came in and asked me if we would come and discuss with him the funeral arrangements.

"When he left the room, I took one more look at you and started to leave, but I stopped. To this day, I don't know what it was that made me turn around and look at you again, but we are so glad I did. I walked back over to where you were, and I started yelling for the doctor to come back. He heard me and came running. He thought I had gone over the edge when I tried to tell him that you were alive. He took off his stethoscope, and to this day, I will never forget the look on his face. He started yelling, 'She's alive! This baby is alive!'

"Next thing we knew, people were crawling all over the place. They moved you back into the nursery, and your uncle and I went to find your parents. I ran up to them and

Twin Souls

told them that you were alive. After I told them what had happened, they started running to the room where they had taken you. Before we even reached the door, you were yelling your head off. It was as if you were letting them know you were angry with them for not taking better care of you.

"The doctors called it a miracle. They said your heart rate must have slowed down so much that it was undetectable. They couldn't explain why there was no pulse though. It scared them so badly that they willingly jumped to any conclusion about what really had happened.

"In the end, they had to issue you another birth certificate because the other was a matter of record since they had already declared you legally dead. So now you know why the contents of that trunk had to remain a mystery. Until now."

Getting up from the couch, she picked up the tray and went to the kitchen. Following her, they still had some questions to ask. "What did Mom and Dad think about all of this? Did they believe the explanations the doctors gave or did they think there was more to it than that?"

"No, as a matter of fact, they didn't believe it. We four took you children home that night. After we had you both safely in bed, we discussed what had happened at the hospital. We sat right here at this kitchen table until the early hours of the morning trying to sort it all out. We all knew you were dead. Even the doctors didn't believe their own explanations, but either they lacked the courage or the ability to find the real answers. So, they just passed it off as your heart rate and pulse slowing so much that they were undetectable.

"What you experienced was nothing short of a miracle. It was so unique. We knew if this ever got out that you wouldn't be free to live a normal life. To enjoy your childhood and experience all there was to experience as a normal, healthy child. We all decided right then and there to never tell anyone about what happened. We were certain that the hospital wouldn't bring it up, because it wouldn't look good on them to declare a child dead and she not be. They were worried about a malpractice suit as it was. So in the end, we all made a promise to do whatever we could to protect you children from that day forward, and we sealed it with all the love we had for you two."

Reaching over, Aunt Kat took both of their hands. "We never meant to deceive you children in anyway. We were just trying to protect you. We never wanted either of you to be hurt. I guess we thought we could always keep it a secret. We probably could have if the accident hadn't happened and your parents had not been killed. Also, we didn't count on Justin turning every aspect of our lives into a science project, either. He gave us our most concern."

They weren't sure what she meant by that. When they looked at her questioningly, she told them to sit back down. "Justin, you always have been an inquisitive child. Even as a baby, you wanted to know how things worked. You used to have a Jack in the Box. It drove you crazy popping in and out of the box. You were always trying to pry it open to see what was inside. You finally succeeded, and poor old Jack wasn't ever the same after that.

"As you got older, you were always taking things apart. You became quite good at putting things back together. Except for the time you put the sweeper back together and it turned into a man-eater. It became second nature for you to find out what made things tick. It became a challenge to buy you anything because we knew that eventually you would take it apart. It wasn't really a surprise to any of us when Jerica had her first accident. We knew then that curiosity would get the better of you."

Finally, Jerica and Justin were going to get the real answer they had been searching for. They sat upright in their chairs, eyes locked on their aunt, waiting for what was to come next.

"It was a beautiful summer day. Justin, you and Jerica wanted to go swimming. Normally your mother would have driven you over, but she was in the middle of something very important and could not get away. You two were given permission to ride your bicycles over to the pool. On the way to the pool, a car hit Jerica. A young kid was speeding down the street and swerved to avoid hitting a car and hit her instead. He knocked her off her bike and she landed about thirty feet from the car into a neighbor's yard. Justin, you were the first one to get to her. The lady of the house saw the accident and called the ambulance and the police. Then she came out to help you. She thought your sister was dead and she tried to get you away from her but you refused to leave her.

"The ambulance attendants began administering first aid to Jerica. One attendant yelled to the other that they were too late. He thought they were losing her. You just stood there looking at them in horror. You knew your sister was dying.

"On the ride to the hospital, she died. They covered her face with a sheet. You were totally distraught by the time they got to the hospital. When we arrived, we asked them to let us see her because we needed to make sure. By the time we got through all of the red tape, Jerica was sitting up on the side of the table, swinging her legs back and forth and talking to some nurses.

"It was then that your young mind realized the secret we had tried to hide. You were only ten years old and really didn't comprehend what you had seen, but you knew that it was something. We also knew that from that moment on we would have to watch you."

Looking at her nephew, she said, "You never discussed it with any of us. We had to be careful and watch you every moment. We knew that your inquisitive nature wouldn't allow you to forget what you had seen. We didn't know what you would try to do. Our fears were not unfounded. It wasn't long before you began testing your sister. One time you had her jump off the hill over looking Myers Lake. Do you remember that, Jerica?"

Thinking back, Jerica replied, "Yes, yes I do. Justin told me that if we jumped off the hill, we would inherit all the gold that was buried deep inside the hill. I jumped; he didn't. The only pot of gold I got was the gold cap that was put on my tooth when I had to go to the dentist from the fall I took. Now that you mention it, he did get me into some pretty bad scrapes."

As Jerica playfully took a swing at her brother, their aunt continued the story. "Anyway, after your parents died, we learned through the information from the different discussions we had with various doctors that you had perished in that car wreck. You had no pulse, no heartbeat. Again, this set of doctors attributed it to undetectable slow heart rate and pulse. We all knew what had happened, even you Justin. You knew it. However, there again, you never spoke up. Uncle Jack and I began to worry when you started reading, studying, and researching everything you could get your hands on about death, afterlife, and things of that nature. We knew it was only a matter of time before you tried something again. Only this time we were worried it would be something far more serious than jumping off a hill."

Smiling apologetically at her nephew, Aunt Kat said, "I was in your room one day picking up the dirty clothing to launder and I saw your box of notes. I was hoping that if we hid them away, you might give up your obsession about this. Of course, I was wrong. If anything, you became more obsessed. You never asked about the box, though, and we always wondered why."

Justin said, "I thought I had misplaced it myself and I knew if I asked you about it, you would want to know what was in it. I knew I couldn't explain it, so I never said anything.

"Aunt Kat, all this information is helpful, but we still don't know why Jerica can do this. Have you ever come up with a more reasonable explanation?"

Patting her nephew's hand, she told him they may never get an answer. It was getting late and sleep was what was needed. She was tired and it had been a long day.

Aunt Kat kissed each of them good night, and they all made their way to bed. Jerica found it difficult to sleep. Everything she had learned today was mind boggling. They had so many answers and yet still so many questions. Giving into exhaustion, she finally fell asleep.

CHAPTER TWENTY-SIX

Jerica awoke fresh and rested the next morning, which surprised her considering the day that she had previously. She could hear her uncle in the backyard talking to the birds and squirrels. Aunt Kat was rustling around in the kitchen, no doubt preparing a feast. Just the thought of the food she would be cooking was enough to wake her taste buds and hurry her into action to beat her brother to the shower.

As she was lathering her hair, she thought of Eric and knew she needed to call him this morning. He would be worried. She missed him terribly. At that moment, she knew when she returned home she would confide in him about her secret. She only prayed that he believed her and didn't think she was crazy. She hurried, dressed, and ran down the hall in anticipation of the food she would enjoy.

As she descended the stairs, a delicious aroma enveloped her. Entering the kitchen, she found Aunt Kat just removing something from the oven. "Good morning, Aunt Kat." She reached around and planted a kiss on her aunt's cheek.

"You made your famous cinnamon rolls. How wonderful! What is the special occasion?"

"The special occasion is that my babies are home, and we have no more secrets between us I just want to enjoy you two while you're here."

Taking a plate from the cupboard, Jerica turned to her aunt expectantly.

Grinning at her niece for her impatience, she dished a big, hot, steaming roll onto it and pushed her towards the table. Placing a fork and a glass of milk in front of her, she told her to dig in.

Having smelled the cinnamon rolls as well, Justin come running down the stairs, "Oh no you don't, Jerica Dawn. You don't get to eat those all by yourself. Move over, I'll match you bite for bite!"

Laughing at the two of them, Kat handed him a plate. "This sounds just like old times. You two were always trying to outdo the other one. Now hush and eat before they get cold."

Uncle Jack came in the back door. He had finished breakfast several hours ago. He had always been an early riser. Assuring his wife, though, that he could do justice to a roll, she dished him one up.

Sitting around the table, they discussed the situation at hand. Justin told them of his scientific discoveries over the past year.

Jerica felt a warm glow as they sat sharing their secrets and fears as a family. She loved reminiscing about her parents, and hearing the humorous stories Uncle Jack would tell about some of the mischievous stunts he and dad would pull on mom and their aunt.

After the breakfast dishes were cleared away, Uncle Jack and Justin disappeared, while Jerica and her aunt went to the garden to collect the ripe vegetables.

The men returned to find the women sitting on the front porch preparing snap beans for canning. Justin took a handful from Jerica's pile and began to eat them. He always loved snap beans. He never helped prepare them, just helped eat them.

The afternoon went by quickly. Jerica and her aunt canned the beans and put a few in the freezer. Putting her arms around her aunt, she gave her a big hug. "I love you, Aunt Kat. I know Mom would be so proud of you. You did a wonderful job of raising Justin and me. You and Uncle Jack gave us so much. We never wanted for anything. You taught us to be respectful, moral, and loving. We couldn't have asked for a better life, and I thank you for that."

Moved by what her niece had said, Kat took the hem of her apron and wiped at the tears flowing freely down her face. The men, made uncomfortable by the "women talk" as Uncle Jack always put it, decided to go back out in the garage and see what they could get into.

Patting his wife's back, Jack placed a kiss on her cheek and they left the porch. Looking at each other, the women burst into laughter.

Dinner that night was wonderful. They had fresh vegetables from the garden, pot roast, and, fresh baked peach cobbler. The peaches were their uncle's pride and joy. He tended to his trees as if he was taking care of a newborn babe. He talked to them and nurtured them every season, and every season they produced the biggest and most delicious peaches in town.

Their hunger satisfied, they spent the rest of the evening discussing Jerica. Between the four of them, they finally managed to piece together the truth about Jerica's past.

After getting up and leaving the room, Aunt Kat returned with a sealed envelope. It was yellowed with age and had been sealed for a long time. Sitting down on the sofa, she handed the envelope to Jerica.

Looking at the envelope, she recognized her mother's delicate script. With tears glistening in her eyes, she carefully opened the letter for fear of destroying her mother's handwriting and began to read aloud.

My Dearest Children:

If you are reading this, then the time has come when the truth could no longer be kept from the two of you. Obviously, something has happened to your father and I, or your Aunt and Uncle would not have given this letter to you. I only wish we could have been with you to help you both through what has probably been a hard and confusing life.

I wrote this letter to you children after the car hit Jerica. I realized then that something could very well happen to your father and me, leaving you children to find out and learn all this on your own. It was only then that I convinced Aunt Kat and Uncle Jack to solemnly swear to never divulge any of this to the two of you unless absolutely necessary. Knowing the two of you as I do, it must have been absolutely necessary, especially because of Justin. Yes, you Justin. You and that wonderful scientific mind of yours.

Jerica, I can only imagine what your life has been like up to now. Your father and I never meant to deceive you in anyway.... Only to protect you. We have no explanation for the strange occurrences that have happened in your life. If you have experienced anything remotely similar to what you have gone through in the first ten years of your life, then no doubt by this time, you and your brother are ready for some answers.

150

Your father and I spent many years and thousands of dollars trying to find that answer. We had to do all of this without help from any outside sources other than your aunt and uncle. If we had asked for any help from others, they would have taken over your life and put you through numerous, excruciating tests. We could not bear the thought of that. We wanted you to live a normal life and enjoy childhood.

The closest we could come to an answer is that during my pregnancy, I was ill. The doctors thought it was the flu but never really knew for sure because it was such a strange type of flu.

Your father and I had just returned from Africa. We had spent six months in the jungle. The conditions over there were deplorable. It was unsanitary to say the least. Your father and I, being doctors, treated many sick natives. Most of them had diseases that were unfamiliar even to us. It could have been one of these diseases that caused your unique ability.

There may never be an answer. All we ask is that you forgive us and your Aunt and Uncle for not telling you about this sooner. I guess we had hoped that in time you would live a normal life. I guess we were wrong.

Jerica and Justin, whatever you decide to do with this information, you must know that you have our love and support behind you and that of your aunt and uncle.

Don't ever forget that even if we can't be with you today, you have your memories and always our love.

We love you, our most precious babies.

Mom and Dad

Wiping the tears from her eyes, Jerica replaced the letter back in the envelope. Looking up at her brother, she was not surprised to find tears in his eyes as well.

"Thank you for giving this to us. It means a great deal. It didn't reveal anymore than we already know about this mess, but just to have a last note from Mom and Dad has been wonderful."

The rest of the evening was spent sharing stories of their parents. Their uncle told them about the time the herbalist doctor they had treated in Africa blessed her pregnancy with abundant life. They never really understood what that meant, but they enjoyed the ceremony he performed and the costumes they wore.

Finally calling it a night, they headed off in the directions of their rooms. Exhausted from all the day's activities, Jerica fell instantly asleep. Unlike his sister, Justin was fully awake, his mind racing with all the new information he had learned today. He was sure that something they learned today would be the key to unlock this mystery.

CHAPTER TWENTY-SEVEN

The next morning found Aunt Kat in the kitchen as usual. This morning she was preparing a picnic hamper, and as she loaded it up, she told Jerica this was for their snack on the drive home.

Jerica realized she was looking forward to going home. She could hardly wait to see Eric. She missed him so much. She had decided to trust in his love, and when the timing was right, she would confide in him. Now she just needed to convince her brother that it would be the right thing to do. She knew he liked Eric, but she was not sure if he would agree to her sharing this secret or not.

Saying good-bye to their aunt and uncle and promising to visit again soon, they left for home. They stopped along the roadside park to eat the lunch that Aunt Kat prepared for them. Jerica decided this was as good a time as any to approach the subject of Eric.

"Justin, I was thinking that since Eric and I are getting so close and it's a pretty good assumption we will eventually get married that I should tell him about me. I mean, maybe he can help. Three heads are better than one, and maybe he can see something we have missed."

Looking at her brother expectantly, she waited on him to reply.

"I don't think that is such a good idea, Jerica. I feel that the fewer people that know about this, the better. I know you two love each other, but your relationship is still new. Do you really think this is something you should tell him right now?"

"Yes, I do. I don't want there to be any secrets between us. He is totally open and honest with me. I owe that to him. I don't want to enter a life with him without being totally honest. He wouldn't do anything to hurt me if that is what you are afraid of. He loves me, Justin. Do you honestly think he would do anything to exploit this situation?"

"No, I don't. I know he loves you Jerica. I know he wouldn't do anything to hurt you either. He has proven himself on that account. He is very protective of you. I'm just afraid this thing could get out of hand. That's why our parents, aunt, and uncle chose to keep this thing a secret. To protect you. To protect us. Look, if you feel the need to confide in him, go ahead. Just be sure you are doing the right thing. Let's clean up and get going."

Grabbing wrappers and papers, he tossed them in the garbage can. She could tell that he was upset with her, but she felt she was doing the right thing. She realized with sadness that this was the first time she could remember them ever disagreeing on something.

As they pulled into their driveway, Charlie met them as usual at the door.

"Hi Charlie old boy. Did you miss us? I bet you're hungry." When they opened the door, Charlie darted straight to the kitchen.

Justin unloaded the car as Jerica fed and watered Charlie. When she was finished, she went to listen to their messages. Justin had three calls from three different girls, and she had six business calls and five calls from Eric. She was just picking the telephone up to call him when she heard voices from outside.

Going to the front door, she found Eric helping her brother unload the car. "Hi, I was just going to call you."

Rushing to her, Eric grabbed her and kissed her. "Sorry, I couldn't wait for your call. I dropped by on the off chance that you were home." Depositing the luggage by the door, he took her in his arms, "I've missed you. Promise me you won't leave me again."

Laughing she said, "Wow, we were only gone three days. If you act like that over that short of time, I think I'll stay away a whole week and see what I get."

Kissing her again, he looked at her, "No way, woman. That is the last time I intend to be separated from you. I haven't been able to eat or sleep since you left. Do you want to be responsible for creating a walking, anorexic zombie?"

"No, of course not. I promise never to leave you again. In fact, I wouldn't want to. I missed you too much. Come on, let's make some coffee."

Releasing her, he followed her to the kitchen. "How was your trip? How are your aunt and uncle doing?"

Turning from the stove, she told him that they were fine. "I do have something important I want to discuss with you later. Please don't ask any questions right now. Don't deny that you weren't going to. I saw that lawyer look come over your face. Right now all I want to do is enjoy your company."

Filling three cups, she handed one to him and yelled for her brother to come and get his.

Over dinner the three of them laughed and chatted happily. Eric could tell there was an undercurrent of tension between Justin and Jerica but he felt it was not any of his business. He figured that as brothers and sisters go they probably had a disagreement over some trifle matter and it would blow over eventually. Of course, never having any siblings, he was not sure if that is how it went or not. Especially a brother and sister who were as closely linked as these two were.

It was getting late and they were reluctant to leave each other. They knew they had to get up early for work, but they were greedy for their time together. Justin had long since gone to bed and this afforded them some private time together.

Taking her in his arms, he kissed her deeply. Pulling away, he looked into her eyes. "Jerica, you know how I feel about you, don't you?" She nodded and he continued. "I want to be with you every minute of every day. When I am not with you, I feel as if a part of me is missing. I know our relationship is still new, but I know that this is it for me." Nervously running his hands through his hair, he said, "I'm not handling this very well. Look, what I am trying to say is, I love you and I want to marry you." Looking at her, he smiled like a little boy.

Throwing her arms around him, she smothered his face with kisses. She was laughing and crying at the same time.

Looking at her he asked, "Is that a yes?"

"Yes! Yes! I'll marry you."

She wanted to share this news with her brother. Grabbing his hands, she pulled him down the hallway and bursting into her brother's room, she startled him awake.

"Justin, wake up! We want to talk to you."

Justin struggled to sit up. "Let me guess. Either you two busted in here and woke me because you need a third hand for poker, or by the silly looks on your faces, you're going to tell me that you're getting married."

Smiling, they told him they were getting married. Hugging his sister and shaking Eric's hand, he congratulated them. "I guess this calls for a celebration."

Getting up, he followed them out to the kitchen. The only thing they could find to celebrate with were three wine coolers. Popping the tops, they each made a toast.

They talked until the early morning hours, making wedding plans. They decided to call into work and skip a day. They knew they wouldn't be able to concentrate. Around daybreak, Eric went home to catch a couple of hours' sleep, shower, and change. He told them he would be back around noon.

CHAPTER TWENTY-EIGHT

Jerica and Eric spent the rest of the day talking about their future. They both agreed to a short engagement. They wanted to be married as soon as possible. They were anxious to start their lives together.

She decided that now was the time to tell Eric about her. She knew that in order for them to share a good life together they must have complete honesty and trust between them. She wanted to know everything about him and, in turn, to tell him everything about her. She just hoped that when he knew the truth he would still want her.

Jerica took his hands in hers and said, "I need to tell you something. I'm not sure exactly what your reaction is going to be. I feel that if we are going to spend the rest of our lives together, you need to know this. Before I start though, please don't interrupt. Don't ask questions until I am finished, then I will answer any questions you have. The only other thing I ask is that you keep an open mind and believe me for what I am about to tell you."

He had known that from the moment he had found her on the beach that she had some deep, dark secret, and now she was about to reveal that to him. He was almost afraid to hear it, and yet he knew he needed to know what it was. Squeezing her hands, he told her to go ahead.

She told him to wait right there while retrieved something from her room. Returning a moment later, she handed him a brown manila envelope. Asking him not to open it yet, she began her story. For the next two hours, she told him about her past and the incidents surrounding the unusual and unique talent her body had. "In this envelope is the documentation to prove what I have just told you."

Opening the envelope, he looked over the documents. Being the attorney that he was, he started asking her questions. "Is that why you were on the beach that night, because Justin had done another one of his tests?"

"Yes, he drowned me. He didn't figure on anyone finding me. He thought I would come to and find my way home like I normally do. He keeps notes on every test that he does and documents times, conditions, nature of the tests, cause of death. Things like that."

He told her that he wanted to see his notes. Maybe something had been overlooked as to why she does this. Relieved that he believed her, she kissed him and told him she loved him. She knew she had done the right thing by telling him. Together they would work this out and, who knows, maybe find the answer.

The week passed by swiftly, with the three of them spending every additional moment examining Jerica's past. Saturday morning, Jerica and Eric went to the library and poured over books on the supernatural and medical facts of African history.

They were covering the same material that her brother had covered in the years of his studies, and yet Eric could not help feeling that the answer was so obvious. So simple.

That night at dinner Justin brought up the subject of doing another test. His excuse was that since they now had more information to use, maybe the answer would be easier to find.

In unison both Jerica and Eric said, "No!"

Looking at her brother, she reminded him of his promise not to do any more tests. She apologized for yelling at him.

Eric also apologized, "I'm sorry, man. It is just that the thought of anything happening to her scares me. I finally found her and I don't want to lose her. I love her so much. I don't want to take that risk. She means everything to me."

"I know that. She means everything to me too. She is my only sister. I just can't help feeling that one more test would give us all the answers. It is just that this thing has driven me crazy all these years. There has to be a reason for this. This is like an obsession for me. I feel the answer is right under our noses. It's like it is there…taunting me, laughing at me because I haven't been able to find it after all these years. However, you are right. We can't take that chance. No more tests."

Taking some of Justin's notes home with him to read, Eric told them that maybe someone who was not as emotionally involved with all of this might be able to find something they have missed. "My emotions are for Jerica, not so much on the test. Who knows? Maybe we will find that, instead of worrying about this, we should just accept it as a gift and get on with the rest of our lives. Which in Jerica's case, could be forever." Smiling at her, he grabbed her hand and kissed it.

The next morning, he called work and told them he would be out all week and to reschedule his appointments. He talked to his father and told him he was going to take a week off and get things organized before he started the big wedding plans.

The explanation he gave Jerica was that he needed a vacation and now was as good a time as any to take it, especially since they were going to be working on the wedding plans.

What he didn't tell her was that he planned to spend the entire week working on this matter about her. He didn't want her to know how worried about her he was or how much more worried he was about Justin. He was afraid Justin wasn't going to honor his promise and stop testing Jerica.

Jerica didn't find it unusual that he would choose to take a week off. The Dexter Pharmaceutical case had been rather intense since they were working on it without the benefit of their star witness, who was found hanging in his cell. He was due some time off.

Eric was sitting at his kitchen table looking through some of Justin's notebooks when he came upon his diary. He didn't know if he should read it or not. A diary was a personal possession. A private part of his life. Maybe it was meant for him to read since Justin himself got this stack of notes together for him to take with him.

After deliberating with himself for the better part of an hour, he decided to go ahead and read it. He told himself that if it was anything personal and didn't concern Jerica, then he wouldn't read it and would return it to Justin immediately.

After skimming through a few pages, he decided it was too personal to read and was just about to close the book when an entry caught his eyes.

It read, "June 12, 1985, 12:45 AM I have just completed a third test on Jerica. I know this sounds morbid, but I have just murdered my sister. I strangled her. I know she is dead.

She has no heartbeat or pulse and she is beginning to turn blue. There are marks on her neck where I squeezed the life out of her. I sit here next to her, waiting, watching, for I know that it is just a matter of a short time before she will sit up and talk to me."

Another entry was made. "1:37 AM She is starting to come around. She has just let out a low moan. Her eyes are open and now she is staring at the ceiling. She is looking at me and just asked me why she is lying on the floor. She did it again!"

The next entry was at 3:45 AM "I have awakened with a terrible headache. It has been sometime since I have had one of these. In fact, I think the last time I had one of these was when I tested Jerica the last time. I have taken two aspirin but they don't seem to be helping. Tomorrow I will call the doctor and have my prescription for pain medication refilled. I guess the tension and the excitement from testing Jerica again have gotten to me. I know it did the last time I tested her. By the way, she is fine. She got up from the floor and has acted normal since. She said she doesn't feel any different than she did before the test. I wish I could say the same for myself."

Something about that bothered Eric. He didn't know what exactly, but he felt it was an important clue. He took up a notebook and pen and made a note to talk to Justin about that. He picked up the diary again and continued reading through it. He was looking for more entries about other tests. He found them.

Categorizing each test as Justin had done, he even went one step further and put the conditions of the weather that day. He managed this by what information he could get from Justin's notes. He also used the weather almanac that his uncle, a meteorologist for the local news station, was able to loan him.

During the days, he spent most of his time pouring over the notes and researching the information that he accumulated for them. His nights he spent with Jerica. Making wedding plans, they shared their hopes and dreams for a happy future.

One particular evening as the three of them sat talking, Justin mentioned he had purchased a handgun. Seeing the surprise on the other two's faces he went and got it and showed it to them. He told them that he was going to take up target practice since he had so much time on his hands and it was something he had always wanted to do. He invited Eric to join him at the firing range sometime.

"No thanks. I have never been overly fond of guns. You do the practicing and I'll admire your courage to handle one of those things."

As Eric lay in bed that night, the conversation came back to him. Unfortunately, he missed the underlying message that should have been clear for all to see. Although Justin had previously been employed, he hadn't missed a chance on doing research on his sister. In fact, his obsession had become more pronounced now that he was unemployed and had the time to put all his energy into it.

Eric's sleep was troubled. It was plagued with dreams of Jerica, Justin, and death.

CHAPTER TWENTY-NINE

The next few weeks were hectic. Eric returned to work, but he still kept pouring over all the notes and data he had acquired on Jerica.

He and Jerica continued making wedding plans and decided on a fall wedding. After making the guest list for both sides, they realized there was no way to keep this a small, simple affair. Among all of their family, friends, and work associates, they had a guest list of over 300 people.

They considered the possibility of eloping but quickly decided against that for obvious reasons: Aunt Kat, Uncle Jack, and Eric's father. Neither of them wanted to hurt anyone's feelings.

Jerica knew that her aunt had been looking forward to this for a long time. She and her aunt had spent several wonderful moments talking about how her dress would look, what kind of man she would eventually marry, and what kind of cake they would have.

After all the possibilities, they agreed to go ahead with the traditional ceremony. Since the guest list seemed endless, they decided to go all out and have a huge wedding with all the trimmings. Since money really wasn't an issue, they decided not to spare any expenses.

Eric asked Justin to be his best man. It surprised and pleased Justin. He accepted and walked around the remainder of the day feeling very proud of himself.

Uncle Jack, of course, would be giving her away, and Aunt Kat said she would see to the catering and wouldn't have it any other way. She said she was not about to leave the most important day of her baby's life in the hands of a bunch of strangers.

Jerica asked her secretary Samantha, who was her closest friend, to be her maid of honor. Her bridesmaids were three other co-workers with whom she was close.

After many hours of planning, it looked as if they finally had everything agreed upon for the wedding. Now it was up to all the parties involved to make this thing work.

Although the wedding was a still a few months away, it seemed to Jerica that she didn't have enough time to do everything. She found herself totally exhausted by the end of each day. She knew that it was a matter of time before she would need to take a day off to recuperate.

She was sitting at her desk, stealing a few well-deserved minutes of rest when Samantha approached her. "Hey boss lady, how about coming out with me and the girls for an after-work drink? You know, just to unwind. I think we all need it."

"Oh, Sam, I don't know. I am so tired. I think I will just go home, crawl into my pajamas, and sleep for the next two months."

Laughing at her, Samantha said, "Come on. Just for a little while. A couple of drinks might just help you with that sleep. We haven't been out with the girls in a long time. Besides, I heard they were having semi-nude male dancers tonight. Now if the drinks don't tantalize you, the dancers should."

"Actually, the drinks tantalize me more than watching a bunch of grown men parade around half nude expecting money to be thrust at them. I never did get into that. Ok, I'll go, but only for a little while and only a couple of drinks. But if one single dancer comes up to me and puts his fanny or whatever in my face, he won't get any money, just a good swift kick instead."

"Great! We are supposed to meet the rest of the gang there right after work. Could I ride with you? My car is in the shop."

"Sure, let's get this mess cleaned up and maybe we can get out of here on time tonight. I have to run over to the credit department for a few moments. They managed to louse up Mr. McCruger's account." Giving a small salute, Sam left the office.

Samantha jumped to the telephone to call the steno pool and let them know that everything was a go. "Tara, its Sam. She is coming. I was afraid I would have to drag her there. I'm riding with her. I told her my car is in the shop. Have one of the other girls drive it over for me. Look, I'll have her stop by the store on the pretense of needing to purchase something and that should give you a few extra minutes to get everything ready. See you there." Smiling to herself as she hung up, she complemented herself on her cunning ability to manipulate her boss into a fun evening.

When they arrived at the club, Samantha led Jerica to the back room. As they entered the room, everybody yelled, "Surprise!" Jerica was so stunned she was speechless. She had no clue that she was going to her own bridal shower.

Looking around at all the decorations and all the familiar faces, she pressed her lips together to keep from crying. "I can't believe you guys did this. This is wonderful! I had no idea. I'm so touched, thank you."

Samantha sat her down in the chair at the head of the table while the waiter arrived with goblets of champagne. Raising her glass in a toast, Samantha said, "To Jerica and Eric. May they have a long and happy life together and be blessed with many children."

Shouts of "Hear, Hear" rang out. Sam continued, "And may each of us single girls in the room get lucky enough to land someone as handsome as Jerica did."

Jerica was opening her fourth gift when a male voice came from behind her, "Sorry I'm late ladies, but I see everything is well in hand."

Surprised, she turned around and lips met hers. The girls had filled Eric in on the details of the party several weeks in advance. "Hi. I'm glad you're here. I suppose you knew about this all along?" she asked."

"You suppose right. They let me in on the little secret awhile back. They told me I couldn't tell you. Said you would try to talk them out of it."

"They were probably right. You know how I am. Look at the lovely things we have." Showing him the gifts she had already opened, she let him open the next one.

"I wanted to be here to pop out of the cake, but alas, I was detained by a drunken client who was fortunate to land an overnight stay in our city's finest cross-bar hotel. Then he expects me to perform miracles and get him out when he is facing charges of public drunkenness, resisting arrest, and assaulting an officer. Oh, and this client happens to be a public defender who just happened to be out celebrating his 40th birthday. That's what I like about my profession, I get all the easy cases."

Laughing, she told him, "Well, you are here now. I am sorry you couldn't pop out of the cake. I would have liked that."

Samantha had gotten them a beautiful, elegant, silver serving-tray with a place where the wedding date could be engraved upon it. The other gifts ranged from small kitchen appliances to elegant linens. The party ended on a high note with everyone having enjoyed themselves and a little too much free champagne.

As Eric and Jerica left, their friends offered the happy couple best wishes and many years of happiness. The waiter brought out a cart to help Jerica load her gifts in the car. Eric helped her stack them into the trunk, and kissing her, he told her he would follow her home.

On the drive home, her exhaustion was finally taking its toll. She decided that she was going to take a week off and catch up on some much-needed rest. She had six weeks vacation available but wanted most of that for the honeymoon.

Arriving home, she found her brother sitting in the living room floor cleaning his gun. He had been at the firing range again. That had made every night for the past week. She found it odd that he had taken such an interest in something he used to refer to as barbaric.

She figured that he was bored and needed something to occupy his time. Gun collecting was the best he could come up with.

The next morning she had to drag herself from bed. She couldn't remember being this tired in a long time. She hurried, dressed, and found Justin in the kitchen making breakfast for her.

She told him about the party and how much fun it had been. He said he had known about it but wasn't able to come. He had some things he was in the middle of doing.

"It seems that everybody but me knew about this. Usually nothing goes on in that office that I don't know. I am surprised they were able to pull this off. Usually, with that many women in one office, somebody lets something slip. I'm impressed."

He knew how the girls in her office gossiped. It had been one of his sister's pet peeves since she began working there nine years ago. He could see why his sister had been impressed that they had been able to keep the party a secret for so long.

Grabbing a second cup of coffee, she went to the living room to find her purse and keys. "I'm going to put in for a week's vacation today. Effective immediately. I am so tired. All our accounts are current, and now would be a good time for me to take off before something else comes up. I feel as if I could climb into a hole and pull it in after me and not care if I ever saw daylight again."

"Ah, come on sis. You know you couldn't do that. You wouldn't be able to survive if you couldn't see or talk to Eric at least twenty times a day. You know you would just up and die."

Looking at her brother and laughing, she said, "You're right. I would die without him. But then I would just come back to life and do it all over again."

"That's true. You would. I tell you what I will prepare dinner tonight. I'll have it ready as soon as you walk in the door. That way, you can go to bed early."

Thanking her brother, she headed out the door. When she reached her office, she had second thoughts about taking the week off. She knew in her present state that she couldn't do justice to her clients. It wasn't in her nature not to give 100% of herself to anything or anyone.

Her boss didn't have a problem with her taking off. In fact, he encouraged her. He knew she had been working extra hard and putting in extra hours lately and could see that she needed this vacation. He appreciated her as an employee and didn't want to lose her because of burn out.

Clearing up any last minute work off her desk, she knew she could now leave work with a clear conscience. She met Eric for lunch at their favorite French restaurant and told him that she was now officially on vacation for a week.

"That's good. You needed the time off. Between the wedding preparations and all the work research we have been doing on your condition, it has taken its toll. Plus, we are with each other until midnight every night. You can't be getting enough sleep. It might just kill me but I won't come over tonight. In fact, let's do this... I won't come over for a couple of days. We'll talk on the phone, but that way you can rest, sleep, do whatever it takes to get rested up. Then, in a couple of days, I'll come back over and we can start all over again wearing you out. I just hope I can handle two whole days without you. Anyway, I have one of those boring seminars to attend."

"Oh, lucky you."

"Yeah, lucky me. Anyway, that will give you the time you need. Now, kiss me quick and let's get out of here. I've got to be in court in about twenty minutes and you need to go home and take a nap."

Kissing her, Eric walked Jerica to her car, promising to call as soon as he got home.

After running her errands and doing a little bit of shopping, she arrived home later that evening to find that dinner was indeed on the table. Her brother had put a nice pot roast together with all the trimmings in the crock-pot. He also written a note telling her that he was at the library and would be home later and to get some rest. With exhaustion taking its toll, she forgot all about the pot roast warming in the crock-pot. She kicked off her shoes and collapsed, still dressed on her bed.

CHAPTER THIRTY

Since Eric had not planned to see Jerica for a couple of days, it gave him some additional time to do some more research. An uneasy thought had been lingering in the back of his mind. He had begun to believe that Justin, not Jerica, was the key to this whole situation.

He started compiling a list of all the things he knew about Justin. His likes, dislikes, age, habits, hobbies, and medical history, as he knew it from the notes he had.

Under hobbies he listed experiments, tennis, and guns. The latter hobby was what bothered him the most. He had agreed with Jerica that a hobby was good for anyone to have, but this thing with the gun had become an obsession for Justin. What he couldn't figure out was why this was bothering him so much. Gun collecting was normal for many men. However, not for Justin.

Taking a break, he went to the kitchen to fix some dinner. The cupboards were bare since he hadn't done any shopping since the incident with the rather large lady and her five children. He decided he would go out and get something.

Just as he reached for his car keys, the telephone rang. Grabbing it up, he heard the voice that always gave him a warm feeling.

"Hi sweetheart. How is my favorite man doing?"

"Better, now that you called, with the exception of missing you terribly. Did you get any rest?" Tossing his keys back on the table, he sat down on the couch.

"Yes I did. In fact, I'm feeling so much better, and I think cabin fever is starting to set in. It is amazing what two days can do to a body. I miss you. I don't think I can make it that long."

"Sure you can. You know if I come over, you won't make it to bed before midnight or later, then you will be up at dawn doing some menial task that could have waited until later that morning. I know this because you aren't the type to sit around and do nothing all day. I rest my case, your honor."

"You're right, you're right. Nevertheless, I still miss you. Besides, I'm lonely; Justin went out for awhile. He said he had some footwork to do on my case. In fact, he said that tonight would be the night that he would finally have all the answers and would see me in a little while. I guess he was going to the firing range again because he took his gun with him."

Eric felt another stab of uneasiness at that information. "Look babe, I'm going to run to the market and grab a few things we'll need since you will be over here helping me redecorate this weekend. I'm also going to grab something to eat while I'm out. I'll give you a call when I get back in. Now, what are you going to do the rest of the evening?"

"Actually, I'm going to do something I never have any time to do. I am taking a long, hot, relaxing bubble bath, and I am staying in there until my fingers and toes are wrinkled. Then I am going to read a book that I have been trying to finish for months and then go to bed."

Eric told her that sounded like a plan and he would call her as soon as he got back home. Hanging up, he left for the store and Jerica headed for her bath.

When he arrived home, he called her as planned, and after a short discussion, she told him that she was tired and ready for sleep after that long relaxing bath. He told her goodnight and he loved her. Then they hung up.

After putting away his groceries, he sat down to study again. He wasn't exactly sure when he found the answer, but suddenly a pattern was taking shape. Grabbing Justin's diary, he started from the beginning. After the first test, he had developed a headache. The second and third were the same, only the headaches seemed to be more severe. After looking back at all the tests, he realized what was happening.

Looking through the papers again he knew that he was missing something. It took him about thirty minutes to find the page he was looking for. Sitting down, he read what Justin had written in his diary.

"I need to call the doctor for a refill on my prescription. This headache is the worse one I have ever had. I wish I knew what was causing them. The last one I had was the night I drowned Jerica. This one is far worse than that. So far, it has lasted two days. It started the night I put the rat poisoning in her cola. Sometimes I feel as if these headaches are going to kill me!"

Feeling nervous about Jerica more than before, he laid the papers aside and he tried her number. On the second ring, she picked it up.

"Hello."

"Hi baby. How are you?"

"Fine. What's up? You sound funny."

"Nothing, I was just missing you, that's all. I'm sorry I woke you up."

"I wasn't asleep. I made the mistake of picking the book back up and got caught up in it. In fact, I just finished it. I'm a little disappointed though, the butler didn't do it."

Laughing at her, he asked her if Justin was home. "No, he isn't. I don't look for him for awhile. He came home a little while ago and got his silencer for the gun and left. He really is getting into this gun thing. He said he needed to learn how to work the gun with the silencer on it, because it performed differently with it on and the noise hurt his ears. I don't know. You know how I feel about those things anyway, so the less I know about them the better I like it."

"Yeah, guns can be real loud." He wondered why Justin would need a silencer. They provided ear protection at the firing range that he could and should be wearing.

After another ten minutes of conversation, they hung up. He felt a little better having talked with her and assured himself that she was fine. He went back to his papers. He had almost reached the end of another pile when a document caught his eyes. It was Justin's birth certificate. Reading the date of birth, he started tearing through the papers. Finding the envelope that had Jerica's birth certificate in it, he compared the dates.

Pacing the room he started talking aloud to himself, "How could I have not known? I always assumed that Justin was her older brother. She always referred to him that way. It isn't uncommon for brother and sister to look so much alike. How could I have missed the fact that they are twins? Justin is older by two minutes. Why was this never mentioned? Maybe they just assumed I knew."

Realizing that he had just found the key to all of this, he re-read the last entry in Justin's diary again.

He had found the answer. He was sure of it. After shuffling through some more papers, he saw the pattern more clearly now. After each test Justin performed on Jerica, he got these headaches. With each test, they became more severe, to the point of debilitating him and putting him in bed. Since they were twins, he wondered if there could possibly be a physical link between them? Could that old wives tale be true about twins? That if you cut one twin the other would bleed? If that were the case, then every time Justin tested Jerica, he was in fact testing himself. No, he wasn't just testing himself. He was killing himself. That wasn't possible. On the other hand, was it?

Then it hit him. Justin wasn't at the firing range. He was planning on another test. He was planning to shoot Jerica. That is why he needed the silencer. To keep the noise down so no one would hear the gun shot. "Dear God, please let me be wrong."

Running to the telephone, he dialed her number. After the tenth ring he hung up, and grabbing his car keys, he ran out of the apartment without locking the door behind him. His only concern was to get to Jerica and Justin before it was too late.

Taking the chance at attracting the attention of the police, he broke every speed limit. Jumping out of his car, he ran to the door. The house was dark. Pounding on the door, he prayed he was wrong. Yelling for them produced no response so he tried the door and it was locked.

Running around to the back door, he found it too was locked. He tried the garage door and it was locked as well. Looking in the windows, he couldn't see anything because all the blinds were closed.

Taking a chance that they weren't in there asleep and he would startle them and end up shot by Justin, he broke the back door in. After yelling for them and getting no response, he ran down the hall.

Flipping the light on in Jerica's room, he found them. Justin was lying in a heap on the floor. Kneeling down beside him, he searched for a pulse or heartbeat. Finding none, he turned to Jerica. Panic seized him, as he found neither pulse nor heartbeat for her either.

She had been propped against the headboard of her bed. Eric laid her flat down and tried again to detect even the slightest hint of a pulse or heartbeat. He remembered everything he had read in the notes about the doctors not being able to detect one.

Praying, he was relieved when she let out a low moan. Her eyes fluttered open. Eric was so relieved. Crushing her to him, he told her he had been so frightened. She asked him what had happened.

Before he could answer her, she looked past him and saw her brother lying on the floor. Pulling out of his arms, she ran to him. "Justin! Justin!"

Crumbling into a heap at her brother's side, she cried his name repeatedly.

EPILOGUE

Justin was buried next to his parents. Jerica sold the house, quit her job, and she and Eric bought a house in the country.

After being married in a quiet, simple ceremony with only her Aunt, Uncle and Eric's father present, they took a honeymoon cruise.

Their joy was diminished by the loss of Justin. Settling in their new home, they tried to sort out their lives and finally put to rest what had happened.

The authorities listed her brother's death as heart failure. However, she and Eric knew the truth. Outside of her aunt and uncle, no one else would ever know of the terrible tragedy that took place that night.

Jerica's body's unique ability to rejuvenate itself after death was only possible by drawing her life's energy from her brother. Every time he executed one of his tests on her, her body needed more strength from her brother to keep her alive, thereby stealing his life force from him. The results of each test weakened him, causing his headaches and eventually his death.

It took Jerica longer to recover from each test because Justin's life force was getting weaker each time he tested her. When Justin had planned that final test, he didn't know that he was planning his own death.

Eric and Jerica concluded that since her brother was gone that her life force was complete. Now she would be able to lead a normal life. To grow old and eventually to die. Of course, they had no way, except for one, to know for sure, but they chose never to find out unless something unexpected happened to test their theory. They decided it was time to put this behind them and get on with their lives.

They settled into a quiet, comfortable life. Jerica made their home a haven for them. She had thought that since she was no longer working she would go insane, but the opposite was true for her. She discovered she enjoyed the domestic life. Her days were filled with cooking, cleaning, and finding new ways to please her husband.

She loved to cook special meals for him from the fresh food that she had grown in her own garden, a talent she had passed onto her by Aunt Kat.

This night she prepared him an extra special dinner. She had placed their best china on the table. The candles were lit and the lights were down low when he arrived home.

Looking around, he now knew what she had meant about the surprise that she had told him was waiting on him when he got home from work.

"Hey, this is great. A candlelight dinner with my favorite wife. Now that is my kind of surprise."

Sitting him down in the chair, she said, "This isn't the surprise."

"You mean there's more?"

Smiling she said, "Yes, but let's eat first."

After sharing the delicious meal that he knew his wife had worked very hard to prepare, he complimented her on her efforts.

Leading him to the living room, she sat him down on the sofa. "Now for the other surprise."

"Oh, I get it. You want to make out on the sofa. Hey, I'm into it."

Laughing, she handed him a box wrapped in blue and pink paper with a large ribbon of the same colors wound together.

When he looked at her expectantly, she said, "Go ahead, open it."

Lifting the lid off the box, he reached in and held up a pair of booties. One was pink and one was blue. Turning to him, she said, "I saw the doctor today….Daddy."

Pulling her into his arms, he hugged her and told her that his life couldn't be any more complete. "From now on it's you and me and baby makes three."

Smiling wickedly at her husband, she said, "Well, not exactly. I'm pregnant with twins."

Bio

Rendi Conn

I grew up in Jenks, Oklahoma, when it was a small town and you could walk from one end of town to the other in about 15 minutes. I am the third oldest of four children. I still live in Oklahoma. I am an Okie all the way. That is the slang word for being an Oklahoman.

My dream of being a writer, began at the early age of twelve years old. I spent my youth writing poems, short stories, plays, and songs. All during my school years, I filled a notebook full of these same writings in hopes of one day being published.

I wrote "TWIN SOULS" in 1988 and until just recently decide it was time to get published. I believe that timing is everything.

I believe in God, and surrounding myself with the people I love most, my husband, children, grandchildren, family, friends and my mother, who truly is my best friend.

To purchase a copy of this book go to:

www.RendiConn.com

Contact Information
Rendi Conn
P.O. Box 91
Inola, Oklahoma 74036
rendiconn@hotmail.com

bush
PUBLISHING
& associates
www.BushPublishing.org